THE BOOKIE

A BRATVA ROMANCE

RENEE ROSE

RENEE ROSE ROMANCE

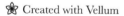 Created with Vellum

WANT FREE RENEE ROSE BOOKS?

epilogues, special pricing, exclusive previews and news of new releases.

Nikolai

There's just no pleasure in delivering a good beat-down anymore.

As bookie for the Chicago bratva, it's part of the job, but my heart isn't into it. Not with this kid.

I bury my fist in Zane's soft belly and watch as he doubles over, wheezing. We're in his dorm room at Northwestern. I told his roommate to take a hike unless he wanted me to beat his face in too.

"I'm sorry. I'll get your money. I promise," he gasps.

"Nah. We're past your promises," I tell him. "This time, I'm here to collect." It's not like he hasn't been warned. The truth is, I probably have gone way too easy on him because I like Zane.

He's smart. Was a decent addition to my poker table before he got into blow and started acting like a douche.

Oleg, our bratva cell's enforcer, hauls him back to his feet and holds him up for me to punch again. I tip my head at Adrian, one of our soldiers, to have him deliver the blow.

I don't get off on violence. Not the way Pavel, the most sadistic in our bratva cell, does. But he moved to Los Angeles to be with his actress girlfriend, who gets off on his sadistic ways. And Oleg, our huge, silent enforcer, is also in love, which has softened him.

The guy was probably always a teddy bear under the huge fearsome exterior, but he pulls punches more often now. Case in point—he's doing the holding up instead of the punching. Considering one aptly delivered blow from Oleg's giant fists could end a guy, it doesn't make sense.

"I've given you slack while you get the money together, but you missed last week's payment. Didn't answer my texts. So here is what's going to happen."

Adrian punches his jaw then delivers a left uppercut to the ribs. Our new cleaner shows promise. Adrian's new to this country and has known great hardship. He still rides the sharp edge of violence. The rest of us have grown softer living large in America.

"You're going to give me the keys to your Mustang and sign over the title."

Zane gapes at me, eyes bugging out. Blood runs from both his nostrils and his lip. "You can't...I..." I raise my brows, and he finishes with a simple "*fuck*."

Adrian hits him again.

"I'm not completely heartless. I'll deduct the full resale value from what you owe the bratva. It's a 2018?"

Adrian hits him before he can answer, and Zane drops to his knees. "No more," he wheezes.

"Get me the title."

"Here are the keys." He shoves his hand in his pocket and pulls them out. "The title is at my sister's place. I'll bring it to you Friday."

I take the keys. "Nah. We'll go get it now—together. I

wouldn't mind meeting Big Sister. What's her name again? Chelle?"

Zane's eyes go wild, not missing my intended implication. "Leave my sister out of this. I'll get you the title right now. Just give me a lift over there."

"Let's go." I spread my hands.

Oleg hauls Zane to his feet, but he stumbles on his way to the door, like he can't remember how to walk. We flank him as we head down the hall, taking the stairs instead of the elevator.

I'd scoped the location of the Mustang when we arrived, so I go straight to it now and get behind the wheel. Adrian shoves Zane toward the back seat and takes the front passenger side.

Oleg leaves to drive the SUV we came in.

Zane lunges between the seats and points to the glove box. "There are napkins in there," he grunts. "Unless you want me to bleed all over your new car."

"Someone else's new car," I say mildly, lifting my chin at the glove box to let Adrian know it's okay to get them. "You think I want to drive your old set of wheels?"

Adrian's lip curls when he hands the napkins back, and Zane flinches at the hardness he catches in our soldier's face.

I drive to Zane's sister's place without directions. I've already done my homework. My brother Dima, our bratva cell's hacker, researches all our players. When Zane got in the hole with us, Dima went deeper. I have everything I need on Zane to wring him dry.

I know he and his sister had an upper middle-class upbringing. Their father was a stock broker who shot himself three years ago. They inherited little because it turned out the guy had a gambling problem. I guess the apple didn't fall far from the tree in Zane's case.

The one thing the dad hadn't touched was his kid's college fund, so Zane was still riding his privilege there. The sister is five years older and works for the top publicity firm in town.

I pull up in front of a brownstone building in a transitional neighborhood of Chicago. It is one of those up-and-coming hipster areas where old buildings are being gentrified, but there are still good deals to be found.

Zane gets out and punches a code in at the door, then leads us up three flights of stairs. "You have the key," he mumbles at me. I hand him his keyring, and he finds the right one and pushes it in the lock.

The apartment is small but nice. Worn oak flooring, walls painted white except for the random accent in muted teal and plum. There are tastefully framed black and white art photos. Everything is relatively neat. I stop and pick up a framed picture of what looks like Zane's high school graduation. He's in his cap and gown, a young woman tucked under one arm.

"Is this Chelle?" The woman is much smaller than him, but they share the same facial features—the shape of their nose and mouth, their coloring.

"Leave her out of this," Zane snarls.

I don't comment. I have no intention of harming his sister, but I'm not above making him think I will. I learned the art of intimidation from Ravil, our *pakhan*. I know it's more what you don't say, what you merely imply, than what you really do. Let their imaginations run wild. Let them wonder how much we are actually capable of. The truth is, while we may operate on the wrong side of the law for many of our business operations, there's still a code we live by. Harming innocent women isn't something we do.

I bring the photo closer to my face to inspect it. Chelle is actually quite lovely. She's petite—I doubt she's much taller than five feet and everything about her is diminutive. Her dark brown hair cascades in long waves over her shoulders, and there's a smattering of freckles across her nose. I can't tell if it's just the way the light hits her eyes in the photo, but her irises appear less hazel than Zane's and more golden.

Zane's gone to a filing cabinet in the small nook of the living room that she appears to use as an office and is rooting through it. "I mean it. Chelle has nothing to do with this."

I'm glad Zane isn't a complete douche. His desire to protect his sister from his foibles scores a few points with me.

"Did you find the title?"

Zane is tearing file folders out, rooting through them, and tossing them on the floor. Eventually, he stands. "Here it is."

He limps over and thrusts the title under my nose.

"Sign it," I instruct him.

"It will have to be notarized."

I smirk. "I'll take care of that."

"Can you just keep it and give it back to me when I pay you off?"

"No. I need cash. Consider yourself lucky that I'm willing to handle this transaction for you. Me giving you full value is a fucking gift, so show some appreciation and get me the rest of my money."

"I will, I will." Zane picks up a pen and signs it over to me. I hold my palm out for the keys, and he unwinds the car key from the ring. "I'm sorry, man. I will get the rest of it."

I pocket the key and drop a hand on his shoulder. "You are very smart. I know you can figure this shit out. I'll expect another payment by next Friday, and if I don't hear from you, we won't be so kind as we were today." I make a point of glancing back at the photo of his sister. "I wouldn't mind involving Chelle in the next transaction. She looks like a hot one."

Zane makes a choking sound, but we're already making our exit.

He can find his own ride back to the dorms.

CHELLE

"I need you to work on the media buys for these two new clients," my boss, Janette, tells me, dropping two file folders on my desk at six o'clock.

There goes tonight's spin class.

Despite my position as a glorified secretary, I'm grateful to be her assistant. As the founder and head of Image First Publicity, she's a bad-ass publicist, turning her minority-owned business into a multiple seven-figure enterprise within three years.

That's why I'm here long past five, when my day is supposed to end. I don't leave until she does because I'm trying to prove I'm worthy of an assistant publicist position with my own accounts.

I love the job. I find publicity both fascinating and glamorous. I definitely have aspirations of running my own firm someday. But to do that, I have to work from the ground up, which means when Janette snaps, I run. Because this business is highly competitive and there are at least a dozen people at the firm who would kill for my job. So for the moment, I'm resigned to having no social life.

Which is fine since my last three Bumble dates were a total flop. I'm not missing much.

Except for sex.

I definitely miss sex.

A little physical pleasure now and then would be nice.

The problem is, I'm not the kind of person who can separate sex from a relationship. I don't know how to date just for sex. I try to picture the guys I date in the vision of what I want my future life to be. It's all very serious, and no one measures up, and I'm left using my fingers and vibrator instead of lowering my standards to have my needs met and then kicking the guy out the door in the morning.

"I will get them all arranged," I promise Janette, who has stopped to lean her hip against my desk.

It's a good sign. It means she's winding down. When she pauses to actually make conversation I know she'll be leaving soon.

"I have potential clients coming in from Madison next week. I need to wine and dine them—show them what's special about Chicago. Any ideas on where to take them?"

"You could always do one of the skyrise restaurants overlooking the city."

Janette wrinkles her nose. "Too stuffy. They're young. It's Skate 3—three Youtube skateboard stars who have monetized their popularity with an online store that's grossing three hundred grand a month. So I need something more lively and hip. What's new around Chicago for nightlife?"

I nibble the inside of my lip. "Let me think about it, and I'll make you a list of possible options."

Janette rewards me with a smile and a quick tap of her manicured fingers on my desk. "That would be great. I knew you'd have some ideas. You're young and out on the scene more than I am."

I don't disabuse her of the notion that I actually have a social life. I mean, I would *like* to have a social life. I partied a little in college with my roommate Shanna. But after my dad's suicide, I pretty much packed that side of me up and shoved her in a box.

These days my social life consists of going to happy hour on Wednesdays when Shanna works the bar and seeing my younger brother, Zane, once a week for dinner, except he's flaked the last couple of weeks. I'm afraid he may be partying too much. His grades last semester were definitely down.

The thought of him ending up like my dad keeps me up at night.

I start straightening my desk, hoping I've read the signs right, and it's okay to leave for the day.

Janette stands. "All right, I'm heading out. I'll see you tomorrow."

I shut down my computer and follow her out of the building, already starting to assemble the list of possible places she could take the clients in my head. By the time I've ridden the train home, I have a half-dozen ideas. I text them to myself as I walk the couple blocks to the place I rent.

When I push open the door of my apartment, I catch sight of my brother's long body crashed out on my couch. Relief at seeing him is quickly replaced by concern.

"Zane? What's up? Are you sick?"

It's not completely unusual for him to be here. He comes by sometimes to do his laundry, but something feels off about him being here on a Friday night.

I catch sight of his face in the fading light and shriek. It's been beaten. It's swollen, almost unrecognizable.

"Oh my God! What happened to you?"

He groans.

"Zane?" I rush to his side, my heart thundering. "Oh my God. Should I call an ambulance? Who did this?"

The sense of dread coursing through my veins tells me I already suspect what happened. He's into something bad. Dammit. I feared something like this was coming but kept trying to talk myself out of the worry.

"I ran into a couple guys' fists." Zane attempts to sit up, gasping at the effort.

"What. Happened?" I demand. I want the whole story. Whatever it is he's been hiding from me for the past few months.

My brother is all I have in the world, and he's my responsibility. I may only be five years older, but after our dad's death, I became my brother's guardian and the trustee of his college fund. I'm supposed to be taking care of him, and I've obviously screwed up, royally.

Tears burn my eyes. "Zane, tell me what's going on," I beg.

He winces as he draws a breath. "I owe some guys money," he admits.

"What guys? Drug dealers?"

"No."

It's a tiny relief. He's been so off lately that I've suspected he's been using drugs recreationally.

"Bratva."

"What?"

"They're Russian *mafiya*. I got behind on my gambling debts."

"Fuck, Zane."

Goddammit. I *knew* it! I freaking knew it.

I stand up and start pacing. "How much do you owe them?"

"Probably around forty grand now. They took the Mustang today and said they'd wipe the full value off what I owe."

"I seriously doubt that." Loan sharks give notoriously

bad terms. They aren't going to give him full value for his car. "*Who* are these guys?" I repeat, even though he already told me.

"Russian *mafiya*."

"Okay, so the forty grand is before or after the value of your car gets knocked off?"

"Before."

I pace some more. "How did this happen?"

"I've been playing poker with them for a while. I used to win big. But… my luck turned," he says, as if that explains or excuses being forty grand in debt to the Russian mob.

"Your luck turned," I repeat in disbelief. "When did your luck turn? How long have you been accumulating this debt? I mean, is it one night's worth, or—"

"A few months. They stopped letting me in a month ago because I was under water. I've been working on a plan but—"

I cock my head. "And that plan is?"

Zane doesn't meet my eye. He gives a half-hearted shrug.

"So you don't really have a plan?"

"No."

"And how long did they give you to pay off this debt?"

He shrugs again. "They didn't say. I guess today was a hurry-up warning."

"A hurry-up warning."

I go to the kitchen and wrap an ice pack in a towel and bring it to him. "I can't believe this."

He takes the ice pack but doesn't put it on his swollen face. "I know."

"I mean, after dad—" My voice cracks.

"*I know.*"

I can't help it, the tears start falling. I snatch the ice

pack from his hands and hold it to his bruised cheekbone, but he jerks away. "Zane, I can't take this. It's too much, okay? I couldn't deal if something happened to you too."

"Nothing's going to happen to me," he tries to placate me. "These guys aren't that bad. I'm going to figure out how to get them the rest of their money, and I won't play again. Okay?"

I sniff. "How?"

"I don't know. Is there any way we could use the trust?"

"No," I snap. I knew he'd ask me for that. "It's for education expenses only. Do you know how lucky you are Dad left that intact when he died?"

"Okay, okay. Just checking." He tries to get to his feet and falls to his knees instead.

"Fuck, Zane!" I lurch forward and catch his arm. "Come on. I'm taking you to the hospital."

2

Nikolai

The game is in full swing by eleven. We have a suite in a posh hotel where I have one table, seven players. I'm satisfied—the house has already made thirty grand, and I have a buyer lined up for Zane's Mustang.

A knock sounds at the door, and I shoot a glance at my twin, Dima, who's in town for the weekend, as I go to open it. Oleg flanks me, as my muscle. Dima reaches for the pistol in his waistband. We're all more cautious since the incident with the Feds last month. Getting shot at one of my games isn't the way I want to go. Dying young has been a possibility since the day my brother and I joined the bratva, but I'd rather go out in glory than from a pot-shot taken by a trigger-happy kid.

I crack the door to peer out.

"I'm here to see Nikolai," a female voice announces.

"Oh, hell no," I say, when I take in the small but mighty female standing outside. I recognize her from the photo at her apartment—Zane's sister.

She preemptively thrusts her hand through the crack in the door before I can close it.

I may be a dick, but I'd never smash a woman's fingers. I'm also not about to let her into the hotel suite to kill the vibe. I open the door enough to step outside, forcing her to back up into the hallway.

She's adorably angry—all five foot two of her. Her chestnut hair is pulled up into a high, thick ponytail, and her golden eyes spark with fire. Bronze freckles dot her nose and cheekbones, matching the reddish lights in her hair.

Oleg looms in the doorway behind me, drawing her gaze, which I dislike for some reason.

"I've got this," I murmur to him in Russian, leaving her in the dark about what I said, and Oleg retreats and shuts the door.

She puts her hands on her hips and raises her brows. "I'm Chelle Goldberg. Sister of the guy you put in the hospital today?"

"I know who you are," I say mildly, advancing on her, just to see if she'll retreat or hold her ground.

She holds her ground, which I find even more adorable.

"Tell me Zane did not give you the location for this game because that kid does not need another ass-kicking from me right now."

"No," she snaps, thrusting her chin up. "I saw the text message on his phone. While he was lying on a hospital bed."

I roll my eyes. "Zane did not require a trip to the hospital, Freckles. The only thing the ER would do for him would be to hand out some pain meds, which a guy with substance abuse issues doesn't need."

That steals her thunder and her breath. She blinks at

me, like my words gave her an unpleasant shock. A twinge of sympathy niggles in.

Does she seriously not know her brother has a drug problem?

Maybe she's been in denial, and my saying it out loud made it real.

"Go home. Take the pain pills away from him. See if he'll smarten up and get his shit together."

"I came here to talk about Zane's debt." She's lost some of her bluster. She meets my gaze but can't hold it anymore.

I fold my arms across my chest. "So talk."

She makes a show out of looking around. "Out here in the hallway?"

It's comfortable as far as hallways go. Wallpaper and artwork and side tables with heavy pottery sitting on top.

"You're not coming in here, doll. Not unless you brought cash."

She clutches her purse tighter, like I'm about to rip it from her arm. "I came to find out exactly how much he owes. And to see if we could come to some kind of arrangement."

Oh, Freckles, yes. I would definitely like to come to an arrangement with you.

The naked-tied-to-my-bed kind.

I let my interest show in my slow perusal of her body. She's not curvy—in fact, she's a bit on the angular side, but I find the whole package to be alluring. Something about her interested me the moment I saw her photo at her apartment. "What kind of arrangement?" My low rumble holds a seductive edge to it, and her body responds, her nipples protruding through her thin sweater.

She firms her jaw. "May I come in?"

15

Fuck. I definitely don't want her in the suite. But for some reason, I'm finding it hard to deny her.

Against my better judgement, I open the door and usher her in.

Oleg immediately moves in to search her purse and pat her down, and I have to stifle the sharp rebuke that rises in my throat. He's doing his job. Protecting me from getting shot again. I just don't like his hands all over her.

She steals a quick glance at the game going on then produces a fat envelope from her purse after Oleg gives it back and hands it to me.

I take out the cash and count it. "Fifteen hundred off Zane's debt," I tell Dima, who is positioned with his laptop near us to record every time money changes hands.

He nods and types it in.

"Is that enough to keep you off his back for a few weeks?" she demands.

"No, bunny rabbit."

Her eyes flash with annoyance at the pet name, but she doesn't address it. "How much more does he owe?"

"He's in forty grand to me right now."

She makes a little *huh* sound. "You took ten grand off for the Mustang?"

I nod. "That's the resale value."

She digs in her purse again, and produces a set of keys. She unwinds a Toyota key from the ring. "Take my car. It should be worth at least another ten grand." Her fingers tremble when she holds the key out to me.

I refuse to take it. "I'm not taking your car."

She thrusts the key in my face and shakes it, the shaking growing more visible. Her lips tremble, too, although I suspect it's with rage not fear. Certainly not tears. Chelle is a tough cookie, that much is obvious. "Take it," she snaps. "You took Zane's."

"I'm not taking your car. You don't deserve that. Have you considered the long-term consequences of always bailing your brother out?"

Her forehead wrinkles. "What?"

"Do you think Zane will learn his lesson if you keep making sacrifices to keep his nose unbroken?"

Her jaw drops. "So now I'm getting life-coaching from his fucking *loan shark*? You've got to be kidding me!"

I smirk. This woman is cute on wheels. I prop my shoulder against the wall and fold my arms over my chest. "Believe it or not, I like your brother. Before he got his nose into the blow, he was a brilliant card player and an entertaining presence at my table. Now? He's a douchebag, and he's out of control. He needs help, but he's not going to get it if you clean up his messes."

"So you beat him up out of tough love? Was that it?" Her voice drips with sarcasm.

I shrug again. "It's a natural consequence when you stiff the bratva. There will be more if he doesn't get his shit together soon."

Some of her bravado fades, and I see uncertainty dance over her expression. I have to fight the urge to reassure her that I'm not going to dismember her brother. Part of the problem is that I let Zane think we were friendly. I may like the kid, but that doesn't mean he won't have to pay up, one way or the other.

"His other natural consequence is losing his wheels. But it shouldn't be yours. You weren't the one snorting coke and playing loose at my table."

Her eyes brighten with tears, and she blinks them back. Swallows. "He's using a motorcycle now. It belonged to my dad. You could go take that from him, too."

"He can bring it to me," I say smoothly.

"I'll bring it—"

"Uh uh," I interrupt. "Stay out of this. Zane can figure it out. He's a smart kid."

She stares at me for a moment then nods.

I open the door for her. "Don't come back here again," I say when she steps close to pass.

She stops and looks up at me. I have the irrational urge to count the freckles that dust her cheekbones. "Or what?" I see that flash of temper again. "You'll beat me up too?"

"You?" I raise my brows, then allow some of the heat she rouses in me to show in my gaze. "No, Freckles," I murmur in a suggestive purr. "I'll pin your hands to the wall and spank that cute little ass of yours until I hear you beg."

Her eyes dilate, berry lips part. "B-beg for what?" she asks.

I hold in my chuckle. "What would you beg me for, Chelle?"

She draws in a sharp breath. "You're…"

I cock my head when she trails off, expecting an insult with expletives.

"Bold."

My lips twist into a surprised smile. "And you're interested." I allow my gaze to drop to the peaked buds of her nipples showing through her sweater.

She looks, too, and flushes. Her gaze sweeps up my tattooed forearms and across my shoulder to land at my throat. The moment she manages to lift it enough to meet my gaze, electricity pulses between us.

My dick gets harder than stone. She freezes.

Oh, Zane. I just had the most wicked idea of how you can pay off your debt.

Except I don't pay for sex. Nor do I allow it to be used as currency.

I have a personal rule about it just to keep things clean.

Besides, Adrian would probably try to put my head in a meat grinder if he did. He came to America to free his sister from human traffickers, a horrific chapter she's still barely recovering from.

I watch as a tremor runs through Chelle's small frame, but to my disappointment, it seems to shake her back to reality. She pushes past me and out into the hallway.

"Don't come back," I remind her.

She flips me the bird without turning as she walks away.

I stay in the doorway, watching her cute ass twitch as she walks, drinking in all that is Chelle Goldberg. Fiery, adorable, and very fuckable Chelle.

Damn.

I want her.

She's lucky I had enough scruples to let her walk away.

Next time she might not be so lucky.

Chelle

I hit the elevator button eight times in four seconds, fully aware of Nikolai's gaze setting my back on fire.

What just happened?

I'm reeling from the interaction.

The elevator door opens, and I launch into it. Of course, when I turn to push the button, Nikolai's still standing there, watching me with amusement.

Damn him.

I just got my ass handed to me by a mobster. That much I sort of anticipated, but it was the way it went down that shocked me.

I expected Nikolai to be terrifying. I pictured gold teeth, chains around his neck, and a revolver pointed at my head—something like that. And he certainly does seem dangerous. But I didn't expect the suave player persona. The good looks. The charm.

His arms are covered in tattoos, but he wore slacks and a nice dress shirt, open at the throat. No chains. Nice teeth. Perfect teeth, actually, and a Hollywood smile.

Nikolai is downright hot.

What would you beg me for, Chelle?

I'm not sure I'll be able to get that suggestive growl out of my mind. Nor can I banish his threat. He wants to spank me?

Um, yes please.

Even now, alone in the elevator, the memory makes me blush. I'll probably be blushing until Thanksgiving.

I hate myself for being so turned on by those words. By him.

What just happened back there?

That wasn't the most unnerving part. It was the way he talked about Zane—like he really knew him. Like he maybe even liked him. He seemed concerned about Zane's substance abuse problem. The one I'd been hoping didn't exist. It shocked me awake to hear it named out loud.

Zane is into drugs. I'd been afraid of that, but honestly? I'd been avoiding that nugget of truth. It caught me off guard, so when Nikolai gave me his Dr. Phil advice on letting Zane fail, I took it in. As much as I hate to admit it, he may be right.

I can't believe I'm taking relationship advice from a loan shark in the Russian *mafiya*.

The elevator doors open, and I step out. A cold wind blows between the buildings of downtown Chicago, making me wish I'd worn a jacket. I wrap my arms around my waist as I jog toward the parking lot where I left my car. I couldn't afford the rate at the hotel garage—it was astronomical. As I round the bend, I stop and look up at the building, as if I might see through the walls and floors to catch another glimpse of my brother's persecutor.

A shiver runs through me. I was crazy to come here by myself. I'm lucky Nikolai wasn't awful. That could've gone horribly wrong.

All the righteous rage I'd harbored on my way here has dissipated. Now I'm just mad at Zane.

He did this.

Nikolai is right. Zane should figure it out himself.

The trouble is, Zane is all I have, and he's my little brother. My responsibility. If I don't figure his shit out, he could wind up permanently damaged or dead.

My mind flits back to Nikolai's comment about the hospital.

I shouldn't find it interesting or respectable that he seemed to know just how bad Zane's injuries were. He believed Zane didn't require medical care. That doesn't make him honorable.

But it does make him smart. Much smarter than I anticipated. The beat-down he delivered to Nikolai was calculated. Measured. Perhaps a prescribed remedy for late customers.

I don't want to find out what he will do to Zane next if my brother doesn't deliver.

I open the door to my car—the one I'd come here fully planning to turn over to the bratva—and climb in.

Well, I still have a car. I may not have a brother for much longer, but I can drive to his funeral.

3

Nikolai

"Swing your end around that way," I instruct Oleg, who has the other side of the new sofa I just had delivered. I'm moving out of the penthouse suite and into an apartment on the floor below. Living upstairs was fine when it was only the six top cell members living together. It was a bachelor pad, and we lived like kings. But Ravil kidnapped the mother of his child and brought her there to live with us, and Maxim moved his unwilling bride, Sasha, in shortly after. Then Oleg had to bring his girlfriend Story to live with us to keep her safe. Now Pavel and Dima have both moved out of town to be with their girlfriends, so it left me as the only single guy swinging his dick in the wind up there.

"Yeah, right there. Put it down." The two of us simultaneously lower our ends to the floor, and I stand back to survey the results. It faces the giant flat screen television I had mounted to one wall. Like the suite upstairs, my place sports the wall-to-wall windows looking out over Lake Michigan and all the luxury associated with the Kremlin.

Hardwood floors, quartz countertop, the finest fixtures, you name it.

I hired Ravil's decorator to pick the furnishings and wall art, so it looks decent. But I've had Oleg and Adrian moving my shit around with me all day, and I can't seem to make it feel right.

What it lacks is… warmth.

People.

The place feels empty.

The sad fucking truth is that I'm twenty-eight years old, and I've never lived alone. Growing up, I always shared a room with my twin. Then Dima and I were recruited—maybe *conscripted* is a better word because it wasn't like we had a choice—to the bratva before we even finished secondary school. I've lived in close proximity to other people my whole life.

Oh, who the fuck am I kidding? Dima moving away was like having a limb ripped off my body. Dima is the more remarkable of the two of us. He was the boyfriend of the girl who died of cancer in high school. Then he quickly became one of the most useful and powerful members of the bratva with his hacking skills. I've never been anything but Dima's brother. The guy who balances him out. The outward face of the package that was the two of us.

Now he's gone to live with his girlfriend Natasha a couple hours drive away. I'm so fucking happy for him, but I am *adrift*.

I literally don't know who I am or what the fuck I'm doing without him here for me to back up.

Staying in the penthouse suite was too painful with him gone. I thought moving down here would assuage the irritating sense of emptiness I've been harboring lately, but now that I stand here in my lonely fucking apartment, I realize it's just going to exacerbate it.

I need a goddamn hobby.

Blyad.

I have no idea why that thought calls to mind the tits of Zane's sister. Playing with her ripe nipples would not be a hobby. *Gospodi*, I am dying to know what they look like though. Something about her still has me hard a week later.

It was her response to my colorful suggestion of how I'd like to punish her that turned me on. I thought for sure she'd be pissed. I saw what a little firecracker she could be. But no, she'd been intrigued. She wanted a taste of my dominance.

Now I can't get the idea of giving it to her out of my head.

Too bad it's not going to happen.

"You and Story should move into the apartment next door," I suggest to Oleg, who stands perfectly still, watching me. The guy can be creepy like that. He's not just silent because his tongue was cut out. He makes his whole presence silent. As if a guy as big as the Hulk could ever fade into the background.

Surprise flickers over his face, like he hadn't considered it. I mean, it's not like Ravil offered this floor up to us. Who knows why he'd been saving it—all three of the luxury apartments below the penthouse were empty before I moved down here. I was just crawling out of my skin up there, so I asked if there was somewhere else I could live.

"It's getting cramped up there, don't you think?" I ask.

Oleg shrugs and makes a see-saw motion with his hands in the air—the sign for maybe. Then he signs something else. I have to pay attention to try to decipher. I may have mastered

English, but I'm still learning American Sign Language. "Ravil already gave you an apartment?" I ask. Then I realize what he's saying. "Oh, Story's music studio. Right. Well, you can afford the rent if he charges you. I remember the giant duffel of cash you left behind when you tried to leave us."

I'm ribbing him. He hadn't tried to leave, he'd been trying to save his girlfriend from his villainous ex-boss. But the point is, he'd left Story a huge bag of cash when he went to kill or be killed by his boss.

Oleg looks thoughtful and gives me the maybe sign again.

I stand back and survey the room.

"Happy yet?" Adrian asks me in Russian.

"English," I murmur because even though Ravil's not here, we follow his rules. He wants us all to speak English because he says language is power. We use our mother tongue when we need to talk behind someone's back; otherwise, we practice our English. Adrian—our cleaner— has only been here a year and still chafes against the rule. He lives with his sister, Nadia, downstairs, and I seriously doubt they practice English at home. Nadia's PTSD from being sex trafficked makes it hard for her to stretch.

"It's good?" Adrian tries again.

"It will do," I concede. "Come on, you two, we have some debts to call in before the game."

No rest for the wicked, so they say. Being the bookie for the bratva definitely makes me one of the wicked.

CHELLE

Shit, shit shit shit!

I bang my palm against the safe at work. It's eight on a Friday night, and I'm still in the office after a long day brainstorming advertising campaign ideas for a client's luxury ring line. Janette left me to clean up the team's mess, including putting the very expensive, one-of-a-kind designer ring back in the safe, but I can't get the damn thing open.

I try Janette's cell but it goes straight to voicemail. Of course it does. I totally remember her silencing it during the meeting. Crap. She may not turn it back on until tomorrow morning!

What am I supposed to do? I don't feel comfortable leaving the ring here. I mean, I could hide it in my desk or something, but the janitor's here, and if something happened to it, it would be on me.

No, it's better to take it home. I'll bring it back Monday and explain the situation to Janette then. She will probably shit a brick, but at least she'll know how seriously I took the job, and by then, the ring will be locked back in the safe, and she'll have nothing to worry about.

To cover my ass, I text her the situation and my solution then bury the ring at the bottom of my purse and leave the building.

As soon as I'm free from the office, my thoughts go to the events of last Friday night. From what I understand, the Russian's poker game is every Friday, and Zane is expected to show up and make a payment or suffer the consequences. *Not my problem*, I try to tell myself. Zane needs to solve this. I'm actually trying to take the advice of his loan shark.

But my stomach knots up in a tight ball. I pull out my phone and call Zane.

"Hey, Chelle, what's up?" Zane's voice is tight and threaded with worry, which kicks my protective instincts into overdrive.

"Hey, what's the deal with the Russians?"

"Yeah, I'm working on it."

Pretty sure that's code for he has no plan.

"What does that mean?"

"I have a plan, but it's gonna take a few weeks to execute."

"What's the plan?"

"Don't worry about it."

Shit. That's gotta be code for something illegal.

"I am worried, Zane. Aren't you supposed to make some kind of payment to Nikolai every week, or he comes and busts your kneecaps?"

Zane's silent for a beat. "*Nikolai?*"

I hadn't mentioned my visit to the game last week. He'd been passed out on my couch on pain pills, and after Nikolai served me up a dish of therapy about letting him solve his own problems, I didn't think telling him I'd gone running to offer up my car would be useful.

"Shit, Chelle, what have you done?" The panic in Zane's voice freaks me out.

I climb on the El and find a seat, the phone pressed too hard against my ear. "I paid him all the cash I could scrape together last week. It wasn't that much—fifteen hundred or so."

"You—you *paid* him?" Zane is spluttering.

Icy tendrils crawl across my arms at his obvious fear.

"How? How did you find him?"

"He texted the location to your phone. You were passed out, so I went."

"Are you crazy?" Zane practically shouts into my ear. "Chelle, these guys are dangerous. Or did my swollen face not convince you?"

"He said he'd take your motorcycle." I cut to what's important.

"What?" Zane explodes. "You told him about the

Ducati? The title is still in Dad's name, I didn't think he'd find out about it. Why did you tell him? That's the only thing I have to get around right now."

"I was trying to keep you from getting killed."

"The bratva aren't going to kill me. I can't pay them back if I'm dead. Chelle," —Zane gives a huff of anxiety — "I'm not half as confident they won't try something with *you.*"

It takes a moment for that to sink in. "With me?"

"Don't you see? Nikolai was already hinting you were in danger when we went to your place to get the title, so—"

"Nikolai *was in my apartment?*" The sense of violation comes as a total shock.

"I had to give him the title to the Mustang. But the thing is, he already knew about you before we went. So you showing up there freaks me the hell out. He could've just grabbed you while you were there."

Cold spills down my throat into my chest. "*Grabbed* me?"

Nothing about my interaction with the Russian loan shark made me think he'd *grab* me. In fact, he'd sent me away and told me not to come back.

And threatened to spank me. I try not to think about that part. Or the tingles it brings to my lady parts.

What kind of arrangement? he had purred, like he was willing to let me work off my brother's debt on my back. I'd be lying if I said I hadn't been thinking about it non-stop ever since.

Still, I have to believe Zane. He's right—Nikolai gave him all those bruises. To imagine he's anything but a monster would be a mistake.

"You need to bring him the motorcycle. Tonight. Don't mess around with these guys, Zane. I'm scared."

"Yeah, okay." I think my admission of fear is what convinces him. It wasn't his big sister telling him what to do, it was about him protecting me from the danger he'd opened me up to. "I need the title, then. You have that one, too."

"Yeah. Stop by, I'll get it out for you. I'm almost home."

"Okay, I'll see you soon."

We end the call, and I try to calm my frazzled nerves. When I get to my apartment I drop my purse on the coffee table and pull the title to the motorcycle. I can't decide between eating or a shower. A shower wins out because if I can squeeze it in before Zane gets here, maybe we can eat together.

I jump under the hot spray and lean against the tile, letting the exhaustion of the day roll off me. Between work and this thing with Zane, the stress is killing me. The image of Nikolai materializes in my mind. Not just how he looked, but his scent comes back to me—some kind of soap with a hint of masculine spice. Earthy yet clean.

Oh, God.

I shouldn't think about Nikolai when I'm naked. The water pelting my nipples makes them bead into fine aching points. I rub my thumbs over them and moan softly. It's weird I can be turned on when I'm so stressed out. Maybe it's my body's hint at how to alleviate the stress.

I should just go with it, right?

I turn my back to the spray and place my hands on the tile, pretending I'm in the position Nikolai threatened to put me in.

What would you beg for, Chelle?

God, I want that accented voice out of my head! Probably if I just let myself get off once to this fantasy, I'll be able to banish it. I bring my fingers between my legs and stroke the soft flesh there. Tip my ass back a little more as if the water is my play partner, and I'm presenting it. I mentally undress Nikolai. I saw glimpses of tattoos running up his arms. How far do they go? Just the forearms? All the way across his chest? Are his shoulders as muscled as they appeared under that crisp button-down?

I grind my fingers over my clit, my breath growing short. What would it be like if I would let myself hook up with someone? No strings. Just sex. Someone like the Russian bad boy loan shark who wants to spank me?

I thrust my fingertips inside and come. The heat from the water and steam make me suddenly lightheaded, and I lean into the tile for support.

A knock on the bathroom door makes me shriek in surprise. "Chelle? It's me."

Zane.

I shut off the water. "Hey. I'll be out in a minute."

"That's okay, I'm heading out. Got the title. Bye!"

Oh. Well there goes my dinner date. Not that he would've made a good one. I would've just been preoccupied with his problems the whole time anyway. I step out of the shower and wipe the fog from the mirror, staring at my naked body.

Huh. I still want sex.

With the bad boy Russian.

I must be out of my mind.

4

Nikolai

It's Friday. I require a payment from you before ten, I text Zane as we're setting up for the game. Dima's back in town for the weekend, which helps my unsettled feelings.

Zane texts back immediately, *On my way now with a big one.*

A big one. Interesting.

I knew the kid could pull something out of his ass to settle up with me. He may be young, but he's smart and has connections and resources. He grew up with money, even if he doesn't have it now.

Strange that I'm relieved for his sister that he's delivering. I don't like innocents being harmed by our activities. Not that she would be harmed. She tried to involve herself, and I find her a serious temptation.

Zane gives the secret knock twenty minutes later, and Oleg lets him in. I hide my smirk when he shudders a bit, eyeing Oleg's meaty fists. The bruises on his face have turned purple and yellow. He's definitely subdued—that cocky shit apparently got beaten out of him last week.

He's wearing a leather riding jacket, and he's got a red AGV motorcycle helmet tucked under his arm that's probably worth around a grand new. I might be able to get $500 for it, which means I'd give him $200 credit.

"What do you have for me?" I ask, walking behind the folding table we have set up near the door of the suite to check people in.

He places a motorcycle key on the table then reaches in the inside pocket of the leather jacket to retrieve a title and a parking ticket for the hotel garage, which he lays beside the key. "I guess you already knew about this. Probably know how much it's worth, too."

I nod. "2015 Ducati. Valued at twelve grand." I pick up the title and examine it. "This isn't in your name."

Zane gives a huff of annoyance. "It's in my dad's name, but he's dead. I can just sign his name, okay? I'm sure you have some notary you can coerce into forging it."

He's not wrong. We have access to anything we need to move stolen goods.

"Where is the bike now?"

"In the parking garage downstairs, space A 31."

With another guy I might go and make sure, but I have Zane fully under my thumb. He's not going to screw me. He's not prepared to disappear and leave town forever. Besides, I know where his sister lives.

"All right." I look over my shoulder to where Dima sits at his laptop. "Twelve grand off Zane's account."

"What about this?" He sets the helmet down. "It's an AGV. Worth a thousand bucks."

"A thousand new. I'll give you two hundred."

A muscle ticks in Zane's jaw, but he thumps the helmet down on the table. "Fine."

Dima makes note of it.

"Hang on, there's more. This should cover everything."

Zane reaches into his pocket and pulls out a small ring box. I make a dissenting sound, but when he opens it, I am wowed by the diamond ring inside. The stone is big, and the setting is artsy and expensive.

"You steal this?"

Zane meets my gaze from under his dark bangs. I realize he has freckles, too. I mean, I guess I noticed them before, but I pick up on them more now that I've seen how cute they look on his sister. "Yeah," he admits.

"Moving a hot diamond isn't as easy as notarizing a motorcycle title."

"Well, that thing is worth a lot. Whatever you get for it should cover me."

"I doubt that." The ring is spectacular, but it isn't worth thirty grand, especially not hot. Still, he made an effort, I'll give him that. "I'll try to move it. You'll get credit for two-thirds of what I get."

"Two-thirds?" Zane splutters.

"It's a generous deal, and I only offer it because I'm fond of you."

Zane lets out a snort. "Could've fooled me," he mutters.

"Believe it," Dima says. "Nikolai's pulling all his punches with you, kid. Show some fucking appreciation." Adrian and Oleg both glower at him.

"I'm assuming the risk of moving stolen goods." I raise my brows. "Or you can move it yourself and give me the cash," I offer, knowing full well he'll get bent over and fucked in the ass at a pawn shop.

He knows it, too. He shoots me a resentful look. "So we're good?"

"*Da.*" I purposely say nothing more to make his brain work.

"Like… good-good?"

"*Nyet.*"

"Aw, come on with the Russian one-word answers. What's the deal?"

I smile. This is why I like the kid. He's not in any position of power, but he's still willing to throw some weight around and make demands. If he ever gets his shit together, he could go far in this world.

Or he could crash and burn.

Which would be a shame for that cute sister of his, who seems to care a shit-ton about him.

"No payment required next week. It may take me a bit to liquidate the ring. I'll let you know what I get for it and what else I need from you. And you're still not welcome at my table."

He bobs his head. "Okay. Thanks." There's still that note of sulky resentment in his voice. I guess he won't be coming back to my table once he's cleared his debt. Which is probably for the best, but I do miss his presence. Except I miss the charismatic conversationalist Zane, not the coked out asshole Zane.

"I'll take the jacket, too." I'm being a dick. Rubbing his nose in it. Whatever. I let him off easy compared to most.

"What? No. This isn't worth that much, and I'll freeze my ass off out there."

It's true. Autumn has fallen in Chicago and the temperatures plummeted this week. Being from Russia, it's nothing to me, but Zane will be cold in his shirtsleeves.

"Take it off."

"Now you're just being a dick."

Oleg steps forward menacingly and Zane flinches. "Okay, fine. Have my jacket." He peels it off and slaps it down on the table. "Anything else you want? My underwear? Socks?"

I smirk and hold his gaze without saying anything.

He shakes his head and starts to leave then turns back. "How much for the jacket?"

My smile grows wider because I was waiting for him to ask. I could easily tell him it's mine as a late penalty, but instead I shrug. "Fifty."

He nods and leaves without another word.

"Dude, why are you giving him a pass?" Dima asks. "I mean, I liked him, too, but he turned into a douche."

I shrug. "Maybe a little redirection will put him back on the right path."

It's not that I'm invested now because I met his spark-plug of a sister.

Dima watches me thoughtfully. It's hard to hide anything from a twin. "You like his sister." He shoots it out like an accusation.

Adrian and Oleg both swivel to stare at me.

Blyad'.

No sense in denying it. It would only make Dima ride me harder.

"I wouldn't mind taking her in trade for what Zane owes," I admit then hold up my hand when I see Adrian's nostrils flare with a sharp breath. "If she was on board. I don't take unwilling women."

But I know I could make Chelle Goldberg willing. I saw how she responded to me.

It would be so easy to melt that resistance and get her to give it all up to me. Especially because she'd do anything to get her brother off my hook.

But I don't just want a woman who is willing to have sex.

God help me, I'm becoming weak. A total sap. Because I want what my bratva brothers have. Ravil, Maxim, Oleg, Pavel, and Dima.

I want the whole package. I want love.

~

CHELLE

"What's the latest with Zane?" Shanna, my bestie, is on my couch drinking a mimosa. We don't get much time to just chill together since I work days and she works nights. I hang out at The Red Room on Wednesdays when she works happy hour instead of the late shift, and about once a month, we do Sunday brunch at my house. A late afternoon one since she sleeps until noon.

This past Wednesday, I'd told her the whole saga of finding Zane beat up and going to meet with the Russians to make a deal.

"He offered up his motorcycle to Nikolai on Friday. I haven't heard anything since. I guess I should text to make sure he's still alive." I say it, but I don't make any move to grab my phone. Zane was right when he said he's of no use to them dead. If he brought his motorcycle to them, I'm sure they took it, and he's fine.

"So it's *Nikolai* now, hmm?" Shanna teases, waggling her brows. "You're on a first name basis with this Russian loan shark?"

My face grows warm, but I own it. "Nikolai, the scary-but-sexy bookie. And no, he told me never to come back."

"I sort of love him for that," Shanna says, draining her glass and setting it on my coffee table. "It's kind of gallant. Like he was trying to protect you."

"You can't love the guy who beat my brother up. Do I need to show you the picture of his face again?"

"I know, but that's what makes it sort of interesting. Like on one hand, the guy's beating up Zane, but then on the other, he's refusing to take your car and telling you to let Zane fail on his own."

I roll my eyes even though I harbor a similar fascination with Nikolai's behavior. Romanticizing the bad guy is a stupid thing to do. "Well, it doesn't matter because, hopefully, I will never see him again."

"Which might make him the perfect option for a one-nighter."

"Shut up. I don't do one-night stands."

"I know. That's why I'm saying this kind of guy is perfect. Because you would never in a million years actually date him. He is sexy. He was giving you the I'm-hot-for-you vibe. That's the kind of thing you should go for next time."

My stomach twists. "I don't do players." I learned that lesson in high school in the very hardest way.

"*You'd* be the player. You just need to flip the script."

I shake my head. "This whole conversation is moot because I'm not going to see him again."

"Well, if you do, I say drag him into a closet and let him put his tattooed fingers all over you." She wiggles her digits in the air.

I laugh. "You're a dork."

"Yep. A dork who's getting laid when she wants it."

"But not by your boss," I throw back because she has an enormous crush on him. "And also, you work in a bar." I would never want Shanna's life. I mean, I feel like she should get a real job and grow up, but I'm also jealous of it. She makes more money in tips as a bartender than I do at my professional job, which is why she abandoned her degree in journalism to sling drinks.

"And you come into said bar every Wednesday. You could pick a guy up any time. In fact, I dare you to."

"And I dare you to tell Derek how you feel," I challenge, referring to her boss who is oblivious to her hopeless crush.

"We've been over this. Not going to happen. I like my

job too much, and I like what we have. I don't want to ruin it."

"I know, I know. I've heard it all before." I pick up our empty champagne glasses to carry them to the kitchen. I need to work on the ad campaign for that diamond ring, so I can't get too tipsy. I'm definitely a one-drink wonder.

Shanna follows and helps me throw our brunch dishes into the dishwasher.

"See you Wednesday." When we finish, she gives me a hug.

"See you then. Enjoy the rest of your day off!"

"You, too, babe."

She leaves, and I head to my purse to get the ring to study again. I decided this morning that not being able to lock it into the safe was actually a blessing because now I can look at it while I brainstorm ad ideas.

I open my purse and dig around. I haven't left my apartment all weekend, so I didn't bother taking the ring out on Friday. It should be right here…

I swish my hand along the bottom with more energy when I don't find it then yank the sides open wider.

"Fuck," I mutter.

My heart starts pounding. I'm sure it's here. It has to be right here. I never left, and I saw it when I was digging my keys out to come in on Friday night.

I turn the purse upside down and empty it completely.

What. The fuck?

No ring box.

That can't be right.

I pick up the empty purse and search every corner again, opening the small zippered pockets, even though I know it wouldn't have fit in them.

Where in the hell is the ring? I feel like throwing up.

My hands are clammy, my head is feverish. Or maybe that's from the champagne.

"Please, please, please," I murmur as I once more search through the contents of my purse on the coffee table. There's no ring box.

I look at my apartment door. Could someone have come in while I was sleeping? But I keep it locked. That doesn't make sense.

I grab my wallet and crack it wide.

Fuck.

My cash is gone.

How...when...? I gasp, clapping a hand over my mouth, my heart hammering even harder.

Zane.

Fucking Zane.

My fingers shake as I snatch up my phone to call him.

He doesn't answer.

"Zane!" I scream into his voicemail. "Where's the ring? That belonged to a customer at work. I'm going to get fired. I'm going to go to jail. What the fuck?"

As soon as I hang up, I text the same thing, ending the text with words that make me start to cry. *If you don't call me back in five minutes, I'm calling the cops on you.*

He calls. "Chelle. Okay, listen. I'm sorry. I made a mistake. I definitely shouldn't have taken that ring. I was panicked about getting beat up again, okay? And they could hurt you. I was trying to protect you."

Fury races through my veins, exploding out of my throat. "Protect me?" I shout. "Protect me by getting me fired and putting me in jail? Thanks a whole fucking lot!"

"Okay, okay, maybe it's not too late. I just brought it to them on Friday. Maybe they haven't pawned it yet. He said it might take awhile."

"You…" —my brain flits over a million words trying to pick the right one— "*asshole*!"

"I'm totally an asshole. I fucked up, okay? I'll try to call Nikolai."

"Call me back," I order, ending the call. I pace around the room, seething. The contents of my stomach swim around like I ate angry eels.

When Zane doesn't call me back immediately, I call him again.

"He didn't answer. I don't think it's actually a cell number. They probably use a VPN for game communication, so it can't be traced."

Fuck!

"Give me the number," I say, in case Nikolai just doesn't want to answer a call from Zane.

"I'll text it to you now," he mutters and hangs up.

I try, but there's no answer, and it doesn't go to voice-mail. I call Zane back. "We need to find him. Right away. I can't go back to work tomorrow without this ring."

Zane's quiet for a moment, then he says. "There's a building on Lake Shore Drive. I don't know the address, but I heard the neighborhood calls it The Kremlin because only Russians live there. I don't actually know if Nikolai lives there. I brought it up, and he neither confirmed nor denied. I'll bet he does."

"So I'm supposed to find some random building on Lake Shore drive without an address?"

"I don't know, Chelle, that's all I've got. You want me to go down there with you, and we can ask around?"

I draw in a measured breath and exhale. As I do, the movie reel of me telling Janette I took the ring home, and my brother gave it to the Russian *mafiya* plays out in my head. I clutch my stomach. I'm definitely going to puke. Desperation swirls around my head, hot and heavy.

"Okay. yeah. We'd better go down there." If that's the only lead we have, I have to follow it.

"Okay, pick me up?"

The thought of being in the car with my brother makes me want to scream. I will probably punch him in the nose.

While he should be the one pounding the pavement to figure this out, I don't know if I can even look at him right now.

"I'm going to go by myself."

"No way, Chelle." I hear the fear in Zane's voice. "It's not safe for you. Come pick me up. Or I'll meet you there."

"Honestly, you've fucked things up enough. You work on getting the money you owe them, and I'll get the damn ring back. I seriously hate you right now." I end the call then immediately feel guilty for saying I hate him.

I know from my dad's suicide how easily I could lose him. What if he shot himself because he thought I hated him?

Gah.

I shove the thoughts out of my mind, grab my jacket and head out of my apartment.

I have to find the ring. That's the only option here. I'm not losing my job over this, and I'm not going to jail.

Two hours later, I find a convenience store owner who knows about The Kremlin and points me to it.

As I stare up at the beautiful multi-million dollar building though, doubts creep in.

This is nuts. The Russian *mafiya* wouldn't operate out of a luxury building like this, would they? Could running a weekly poker game really net profits enough to afford something like this?

Then again, Zane was into them for tens of thousands of dollars, so maybe it would.

The moment I march in, I know I have the right place.

The security guard or doorman or whatever you call the guy sitting behind the giant curved copper desk is covered in tattoos, same as all the guys I saw at the poker game. He gives me a stony stare.

I attempt to clear the desperation from my voice. "Hi, I'm here to see Nikolai," I say, like I'm at a doctor's office and have an appointment.

He stares back at me without comment.

Shit. I glance around to see the elevator bank behind him.

"Um, I'll just let myself up, then?" I don't know how that would work. Do I plan to knock on every door in the place?

Yes. Dammit. If I have to, I will.

The security guy shakes his head. "You can't go up." His accent is thick and definitely Russian. There's no doubt I'm in the right place.

I want to toss out something reckless like, "try to stop me," but one look at his bulging biceps and menacing scowl tells me he'd more than try.

I swallow. "Listen, I really need to see Nikolai. It's super important."

"Nikolai who?"

Crap!

"Nikolai, um, the one who runs the poker games?"

The guy immediately starts shaking his head. "You need to leave the building."

I take it as good news. Nikolai definitely lives here, or he would've looked confused.

I draw myself up and fold my arms across my chest. "I'm not leaving the building until I see Nikolai."

The guy comes from behind the desk.

Oh fuck. He's throwing me out.

I drop to the floor and sit cross-legged like I'm some peaceful protester from the sixties. "Call Nikolai. Tell him Chelle is here, and I'm not leaving until I talk to him."

The guy strides over and towers over me, his brows down like he's pissed. "Get out of building," he bites out, his accent thick.

"I need to see Nikolai. Please call him."

He reaches down and grabs my upper arms.

I refuse to unfold my legs, making my weight dead weight. Still, he's strong. He deadlifts me from the floor and shakes me to make my legs uncross.

When I still refuse, he shakes his head and starts hauling me toward the door.

"Wait!" I cry out when I realize once I'm out that door I'll have no way back in. "Please. I'll do anything. It's life or death. I need to see Nikolai." I reach out and wrap my legs around his waist like a koala bear, so he won't be able to deposit me outside when he gets there.

"Please. Please. Please just call him," I beg. "*Pozhaluysta*." Unable to keep it in, my voice breaks and tears spill from my eyes.

I always hated girls who cried to get their way, but I see an instant change in the guy.

He stops walking. Indecision scrawls across his face.

"Please, please, please. Please call Nikolai for me. I need to talk to him."

"Put feet down," he grumbles.

"Will you call him?"

"Wait here."

I release the strangulating hold my legs have on his

waist—thank you, spin class, for my leg strength—and let him put me on my feet.

When he walks back to the front desk, I follow. He frowns at me as he picks up a cell phone and dials. He speaks into it in Russian, rapidly and with exasperation. Then he goes silent.

"Is he coming?" I ask.

He shakes his head and holds up a finger.

My heart pounds against my breastbone.

It seems like forever that the two of us stand there in silence while he waits for an answer, then he replies into the phone and puts it back in his pocket.

"Nikolai will come."

Nikolai

I ride the elevator to the ground floor with a semi.

When Maykl called up to tell me there was a small, hysterical young woman downstairs demanding to see me, I knew it was Chelle even before I flicked over to the security feed and rewound to watch.

She's still adorably fierce. Throwing around all hundred pounds of her body to get her way.

I know she's either here about the ring or something bad has happened to Zane. Probably both. Zane could've been busted for stealing it, and she's hoping to get charges dropped by turning it in.

When I exit the elevator, Maykl is still patting her down for weapons, which for some reason annoys me. I want his hands off her. She already climbed him like a tree when he tried to take her out of the building.

"Nikolai," she calls the moment she sees me, launching out of Maykl's grasp and running for me.

Maykl gives me a nod to let me know she's unarmed.

She reaches me and makes contact, her palms spreading over my ribs as she looks up at me. My breath leaves my chest when I realize her cheeks are wet. "Nikolai," she says, again, sounding breathless. "The ring Zane gave you, do you still have it?" Before I have a chance to answer, she rushes on. "It belongs to a client at work. I wasn't even supposed to have it, but I couldn't get the safe open, and I was the last one there. I didn't want to leave it in case the cleaning people found it or something, so I took it home. I didn't realize Zane—the fucker—had taken it until this afternoon, and I have to get it back. I mean, I *have to* get it back. I don't want to lose my job or go to jail or anything like that." Her golden eyes swim with tears. "Please tell me you still have it."

My body is feverish from having her up against me and the need to make those tears stop makes me itchy.

"I still have it."

"Okay." She takes her first breath since she threw herself at me. "Okay. I know Zane owes you a ton of money, and we're going to pay it off, but please, please, please," —she fists my shirt and tugs on it— "I am begging you, Nikolai. Please can I have it back?"

I allow a slow smile to curve my lips. "I like it when you beg, Chelle."

More relief sweeps through her body, and she melts into me. Whether she's just happy because she thinks I'll give her the ring, or if it's her body responding to my innuendo, I can't be sure.

"Please, I'll do anything. I'll be your sex slave, if that's what you're into. I'll give you my car, every piece of jewelry I own. I just need that ring back."

My dick gets harder. "Come upstairs," I invite,

unclenching her fingers from my shirt to hold her hand. "I'm sure we can come to some arrangement."

She allows the intimacy, staying by my side as we walk to the elevators. Once inside, I release my hold, and she backs up against the wall, her hands tucked behind her, her gaze pinned to my face. She's wary but attentive. Obviously willing to do anything I ask of her at the moment.

I'm a bastard for all the dirty ideas flying through my head. Did she actually say the words, *sex slave?*

She'd look so damn cute in a collar and leash. I'd put a butt plug in her ass and make her crawl around…

I stop before I get a full-on boner.

I wouldn't do it.

I'd be an asshole to take advantage of her plight. Still my dick doesn't get the memo, and it remains chubby, hoping for some action.

I shove my hands in my pockets and regard her. She's in a pair of black yoga pants and a long sweater that molds perfectly to her small but proportionate tits. Her dark hair is piled on top of her head in a messy bun. Her generous lips look soft and kissable. I try not to think how they'd look stretched around my cock.

Neither of us says a word. I'm not sure my little sex-slave is breathing.

"I don't accept sex as a form of currency," I finally tell her. I don't know why I let her off the hook so quickly. It would've been easy to make her sweat a few more minutes. Maybe I was afraid she'd pass out due to lack of oxygen.

She bobs her head in relief. "Good to know," she chokes out. "I, um, don't usually offer it."

My lips twitch. "Yeah, I figured. But I sort of love that you went there. Now I'm having a hard time not picturing you in all kinds of compromised positions."

She flushes a sweet shade of pink but is saved by the elevator ding from replying.

The doors swish open, and I place my hand at the small of her back to guide her into the hallway.

"This way, *zayka.*"

"What does *zayka* mean?"

"Bunny."

I let her steal a look at me as I open the door. When I push it wide to usher her in, she stops just inside and murmurs, "Wow."

I thought I was over impressing women with the magnificent floor-to-ceiling views of Lake Michigan, but apparently I'm not because I drink in her shock like it's fuel.

"I guess being a loan shark really pays, huh?"

"Rich boss. He owns the building. I'm just lucky enough to benefit from it."

"Did you recently move in?"

"How can you tell?"

She shrugs. "I don't know. It still looks uninhabited."

I ignore the discomfort that snakes through my belly at her observation. Like the apartment is a metaphor for my life.

"Wait here, little bunny." I leave her in my living room to retrieve the ring from the safe in my bedroom.

"I'm not your little bunny," she addresses my back as I exit.

"No?" I call back from the bedroom. "A minute ago you were begging to be my sex slave. I think you're whatever the fuck I want you to be right now. I hold all the cards, *zayka*, and it's an unbeatable hand."

"Poker metaphor," she snorts. "How fitting."

I walk out holding the ring case up. "Want it or not?"

She concedes, opening her palms and bowing her head. "Happy to be your bunny."

"That's more like it." I smirk as I approach. I stand in front of her, hold the little jewelry box up and waggle it.

She eyes it. "So, ah, what arrangement are we going to come to?"

"I'm still thinking," I admit.

She stops breathing again.

"The forfeit penalty goes on Zane's account because he's the asshole who fucked us both over on this." She starts to interrupt, protesting the increase to Zane's ledger, but I speak over her. "But I will give you the ring for a kiss."

She falls silent. "A kiss where?"

I chuckle. "On the lips. I'm not that crude." I turn away to adjust myself. "You just made my dick hard."

To my delight, her eyes dilate, like she's excited about the kiss. I tuck the jewelry box into her purse because I want my hands free for this, then cup the back of her head and pull her face up to mine. She rises up on her toes, and I have to lean forward to mate my lips to hers.

Blyad'. I was right. They are soft and supple. She tastes like brown sugar or something sweet—it must be a lip balm, and I like the way it lets my lips glide.

Her hands come to my chest, lightly resting there as she tentatively returns the kiss.

I deepen it, prying her lips open as my other hand slides down her back to land on her ass. I help myself, squeezing her soft flesh as I walk her backward.

She fists my shirt as I maneuver her against the wall, where I pin her smaller body with mine. My tongue invades her mouth at the same time I stroke up the cleft of her ass. The soft material of her yoga pants yields to my exploration enough that I feel when her muscles contract.

I fuck her mouth with my tongue as I pulse my finger against her anus. My cock is harder than marble, and I grab her ass with both hands to lift her, so I can grind it in the notch between her legs, reveling in her heat and the way she rides it with her feet hooked behind my back.

I don't want to stop. I want to kiss this girl senseless. Leave her panting and breathless and unable to recall her own name. I want her begging again, pleading to be my *zayka*.

But the kiss was coerced. A mild coercion but possibly still unwanted.

She may be returning it, but she had no choice, really. Not if she wants her ring back.

So I break it.

She stares up at me, lips swollen, eyes glassy.

It's all I can do not to claim that pout once more, except I know if I did, I wouldn't stop with a kiss. I'd pick her up and carry her straight into my bedroom, breaking every rule I have about sex as currency and forcing women.

Reluctantly, I lower her hips, and she puts her feet down to stand. When I ease my body back, she falls against the wall like her legs don't work. I want to steady her, but I don't dare touch her again.

I step back and tip my head sideways toward the door. "Get out."

A laugh tumbles from her lips. "Or you'll spank me?" She seems happy. But then, she got her ring back and didn't have to blow me, so of course she's happy. It wasn't that she needed my kiss. Or that she craves another one.

I smile back because I'm already far too fond of her to play mean. "That's right."

I know the idea excites her, or she wouldn't have

mentioned it again. Of course, I saw her body's reaction to my words the first time.

She walks to the door and stops with her hand on the handle to look back. "Thank you, Nikolai." She seems sincere.

"My pleasure," I say, which is the truth.

She steps through the door and starts to close it.

"But I will break Zane's nose for his fuckery."

She freezes, her eyes flaring wide. "No, please, Nikolai—"

"You have no say in this," I interrupt, and her mouth snaps shut.

There. The fear is back, as it should be. I'm the bratva bookie. I can't let everyone who owes me something off with a kiss.

"And you still owe me," I tell her.

She likes that better. She softens her hip against the doorframe. "What do I owe you?"

Huh. Is she still offering sex?

Nevermind. It doesn't matter if she offers or I demand it, I still don't accept it as currency. I've had enough meaningless sex to last me a lifetime.

I don't need any more.

The next time I take a woman to my bed, I want it to be something real. Like what the others have. Or I at least want to find out if I'm capable of having something real.

"A favor. When I call it in, you'll have to give it."

She rubs her puffy lips together. "Give what?" her voice sounds husky.

"Whatever I demand, Freckles. That's how it works."

Probably realizing I might mean something more sinister than a kiss, she pales and draws herself up from the doorframe. "I rescind my thanks, then," she says. She's so fucking adorable when she gets tart. "Since this is just business."

"Out," I tell her, and she shoves the door closed with a click.

I stand there a moment still staring at the door, a smile playing around my lips. Then I pull out my phone and call Dima.

"What's up, *mudak*?" Dima answers. It sounds like he's in the car, probably with Natasha, since the two are inseparable.

"I need you to dig up everything you can on Chelle Goldberg."

"Zane's sister?"

"*Da.*"

"Now look who's cyberstalking a woman."

Before Dima finally let himself have Natasha, the guy played full-on cyberstalker with her, watching her go in and out of our building, tracking everything there was digitally available on her.

"Shut up, or I will tell your fiance the full extent of your creepiness. I know I'm on speaker. Hi, Natasha."

"Hi, Nikolai," Natasha says with a laugh. "What's the full extent of Dima's creepiness?"

"Nevermind, we don't need to go there," Dima says. "So, you want the full dossier on Chelle?"

"I want everything."

"Give me a couple days."

"I need it tomorrow." I end the call as Dima's telling me he'll see what he can do.

I know the guy can do pretty much anything, and I can't wait to get my hands on it.

I may have let Chelle go, but that doesn't mean I'm finished with her. In fact, I'm just getting started.

5

Chelle

"So? How was the kiss?" Shanna demands from across the bar.

I'm at the Red Room for happy hour, telling Shanna about my visit to the Kremlin. I look forward to my Wednesdays here because it's not too crowded during happy hour, and Shanna has time to lean her elbows on the bar and chat.

Derek, her sexy oblivious boss, doesn't come in until later.

"Hot. Super hot. It was more than a kiss."

"Wait… you screwed him?" Shanna lowers her voice even though we probably can't be heard by anyone over the sound of the music.

"No!" I protest way too loudly. "I just mean, it was a full-on kiss with all body parts involved."

Shanna's eyes narrow skeptically. "So sex."

"No!" I laugh, getting exasperated. Seriously, she's so into gratuitous sex that she can't comprehend why I don't do that. "Like his hands were everywhere, and it went on forever."

"And then what?"

I shrug. "Then he gave me the ring back, and I left." Well, technically he threw me out, but I prefer to rewrite the narrative a bit.

A guy comes to sit down beside me, which is annoying because there are a slew of empty barstools all up and down the bar, and I'm having a private convo with my bestie.

"I think you need to get laid."

Oh for fuck's sake. Did Shanna have to say that so loudly? The guy next to me grins and tries to catch my eye.

"I think you need to shut up." Not my best come-back. I'm flustered by our audience.

Shanna turns and makes eye contact with him. "What can I get you?"

"Grey Goose, neat."

I steal a glance. He's good-looking. About my age. Nice leather jacket, smells like expensive cologne. Obviously looking for a hook-up.

"And whatever she's having." He jerks his thumb my way.

"Oh, that's okay," I say quickly. I've almost finished my first and more than one drink puts me under the table.

"She's drinking a dirty martini because she's a dirty girl," Shanna says, and I seriously want to kill her.

"I'm good," I say, but Shanna makes me one, anyway.

Maybe she just wants to run up his bill. Or else she's trying to help me out in the getting laid department. I steal another glance. This guy is cute, for sure.

But I don't do rando guys, and I especially don't do players. I learned my lesson on that one, don't need to do it again. I'm just not a hook-up sex kind of person.

Oh well. I guess I can tell him that after I enjoy the drink he bought me.

I sip on the martini and dare a glance at him.

He scoots his bar stool closer to me.

Gah. He is good-looking. Yet he does absolutely nothing for me. I take another sip of my martini.

"So you and the bartender are friends?"

I shouldn't fault him for a lame opener. What else could he go with? *So you need to get laid?* Or *Come here often?*

"Yes. We were college roommates. She was the one having noisy sex in the bunk above mine, if you hadn't guessed." I roll my eyes.

There. Show him a bit of my prudish outlook. Maybe that will scare him away.

It doesn't seem to. I drink some more of my cocktail and hope Shanna will return from the other end of the bar soon.

Maybe I should just head home?

Except now I'm a little too tipsy to be out taking public transportation alone. I should sit and let some of the alcohol wear off.

Or eat some food. Too bad they don't have any here.

I pull the toothpick loaded with olives out of my drink and put all three of them in my mouth. The guy watches my lips like it's the sexiest thing he's ever seen.

Hope I don't squirt olive juice on him.

"More olives," I call out to Shanna, who is serving someone else.

"I'm Derek." The guy holds his hand out to me.

"Chelle." I shake his hand briefly, but turn my shoulders back to face the bar, inviting Shanna to return.

"Shell as in Shelly? Or short for Michelle?"

"Just Chelle."

"Well, just Chelle, what do you do for a living?"

I want to think of something really creative, just to fuck with him, but my brain processing has slowed too much. "I am a publicist," I say. "Well, publicist's assistant, really. But I hope to be a full-fledged publicist soon."

The guy scoots his barstool closer.

Dammit. I shouldn't have answered!

"So what does a publicist do?"

"We strategize with clients on their brand, manage social media platforms, that kind of thing." I stay facing the bar, which unfortunately means I'm facing my drink which unfortunately means I drink it all.

Oops.

The room spins. I pull off my work jacket and hang it on the back of my chair.

I'm sure I should ask what he does for a living, but I'm really not interested in carrying this further. I know how it's supposed to end, and since I'm not looking for that end, it's a waste of both our time. I came to hang out with Shanna not get laid.

Where in the hell is Shanna?

Oh good, here she comes. Wait, why is she bringing another round?

"Oh, no, no, no." I push the martini to the far side of the bar. "I've had enough. I should probably get home."

My wanna-be hookup hops off his barstool. "I can get you home safely."

I shake my head and hold up my hand. "No, no, no, no. I'm going to sit a while and then go home." I'm slurring now.

"Well, if you're going to stay, at least have a few sips of the drink I bought you." Wanna-be slides the drink back in front of me.

Someone appears on my other side and a hand slides the drink away again. The fingers are tattooed, like—

"Hey!" I'm irrationally excited. "I know someone with tattoos like—" I look up at the man beside me and the words die in my mouth. "Oh, *it's you.*"

Nikolai smiles down at me with amusement, like my drunk self isn't completely obnoxious. "It's me. I'm going to take you home now."

I turn to look at Wanna-be, slapping the back of my hand against Nikolai's chest. "*He's* going to take me home."

Wanna-be is pissed. "Who's he?"

"He's my brother's—" my brain catches up and I amend, "he's my boyfriend. He came to pick me up because I had too much to drink."

Even in my drunken state, zings of excitement run through me knowing what I've just invited. Pretending to be the girlfriend of a guy in the Russian *mafya* probably opens a door I should've left shut. Am I really going to let Nikolai take me home?

Wanna-be scowls at me. "You could've told me that before I bought you two drinks."

My brain spins off on possible retorts, like, *I said I didn't want a drink* or *I'll pay for the fucking drink, then, asshole,* but Nikolai tosses two twenties on the bar. "They're paid for. Now turn around and walk away before I break your nose."

Wanna-be's eyes narrow, and I realize with a lurch of misgiving that Nikolai would follow-through without the blink of an eye.

"He's not kidding," I say quickly as I hop off my bar stool in Nikolai's direction. "Sorry for the confusion."

"Don't apologize to him," Nikolai growls.

Wanna-be scowls and shakes his head then grabs the money from the bar and walks away, pocketing it all.

"He took the whole thing?" I wave my hand in the

direction of the place where the bills were in disbelief. "If he doesn't leave my friend the very best tip, I will kick his ass myself," I turn and declare to Nikolai, whose lips kick up.

He curls his tattooed fingers around my nape. "You ready to go?"

"Wait, wait, wait. Just *hold* on." I register how exaggerated my speech is but can't seem to modulate it. "What are you doing here?" I squint up at my sexy rescuer.

He shrugs. "I came in for a drink. Saw this guy bothering you and figured I should intervene."

I wrinkle my nose and cock my head to the side. I'm too tipsy to decipher what's off about his explanation but fortunately Shanna finally reappears to help me out.

Nikolai

Gospodi, I wanted to pound that *mudak* who was hitting on Chelle into the ground.

Dima gave me his full report on Zane's older sister a couple days ago, and one of the things he'd flagged was her regular charges at this cocktail lounge every Wednesday evening. I came tonight just to see who she had a standing date with and, then, was surprised to see her alone.

Now, as the bartender gives me a very sharp once-over, I understand. Chelle said the bartender was her friend. This is who she comes to hang out with on Wednesdays. At least, I hope that's the explanation.

It sure as hell wasn't that bastard buying her too many drinks when she clearly can't handle them.

"Hey, what are you doing with my friend?" the bartender demands.

I give her a cool look. "I'm taking her home. She's obviously had too much to drink, which you could've prevented."

The corners of her lips tip up like I busted her. "I was trying to get my friend laid. He seemed nice enough."

"*Shanna!* Shut. Up," Chelle hurls across the bar.

"You have a fucked up idea about nice. In my book, getting a woman too drunk to refuse is akin to forcing her."

The bartender continues to smirk, like her friend's safety is all in good fun. "You must be Nikolai?"

Something moves in my chest.

Chelle was talking about me? With her friend?

I shouldn't be so satisfied about that fact, but I am.

"Yep," Chelle answers for me, putting her hand on my chest and leaving it there. "This is the infamous Nikolai." She pats me, and I have to resist the urge to catch her fingers and kiss them. "Beater-Upper of Brothers."

"Uh huh. So I'm thinking you don't really have that much room to get judgey with me." Chelle's friend folds her arms and raises her brows. "Beater-Upper of Brothers."

"A discussion for another time, perhaps." I turn Chelle to face the door. "Does she owe you anything?"

"Nope. Have fun!" There's a gleeful tone in her voice that implies I'm about to do the same thing that *mudak* hoped to do with Chelle, and it irritates me.

But then Chelle hooks her arm through mine, using me to help balance her as she weaves through the tables to the door, and I forget it all.

Maybe I'm not pissed that asshole got her drunk because it gave me this chance to see her with her guard down. Find out what's under the surface of Chelle's fiery personality.

I lead her to where I parallel parked my new Tesla S

61

and open the passenger door. "Oh my God, you have a Tesla?" she gushes as she climbs in. "I love Teslas! I totally want one. Where do you charge it?"

"In the garage of my building," I say before I shut the door.

She's a fun drunk, for sure. As much as I love the woman with attitude, I love this friendly version even more. Especially because I know she usually keeps it buttoned up.

"I'm sorry my friend said she was trying to get me laid," she slurs when I climb behind the wheel and merge into traffic. "She's ridiculous. I mean, completely ridiculous. She knows I don't do casual sex, but she works in a bar, so that's pretty much all she sees or does. She seems to think it would solve everything for me."

"What needs solving?" I ask.

"Well—" She pauses and looks over at me, her lips parted. Then she shakes her head quickly. "Um, nothing. Nothing at all. That's the thing. I don't need fixing." She holds her palm out like a stop sign. "And I definitely don't do players."

"Who are you referring to?"

"*To whom*," she corrects then winces. "Sorry. I'm so sorry. I shouldn't correct your English. I'm such a bitch."

"Why not? I would correct your Russian. It's fine. *To whom* are you referring? Me?"

"Oh God," she moans and covers the half of her face closest to me with one hand.

"You think I'm a player, Chelle?"

"Well, obviously."

I can't decide why that irritates me. "Why do you think so?"

She removes her hand and gives me an up and down look. "The way you dress, your innuendos, the, um, thing you said to me."

I can't resist a half-smile.

"I'm not a player," I tell her, even though it's a lie. My entire relationship history has been a series of one-night stands.

She doesn't buy it. Her look would be withering if she were sober, but drunk, it's just adorable. "You are totally a player. How many serious girlfriends have you had?" she demands.

I tighten my lips and keep my gaze on the road.

"Aha! None, am I right?"

"My profession hasn't lent itself to relationships. They were forbidden."

Even drunk, Chelle is smart enough to pick up on the tense I used. "*Were?*"

I shrug. "There were rules against it. Rules with deadly consequences. But my boss has eased them."

"Your boss with the fancy building?"

"That's right." I pass her apartment and find a parking spot a half a block away.

She looks around animatedly as I let the Tesla do the parallel parking. "Wait, how did you know where I lived?"

"I've been here before, Freckles. To get the title to Zane's car."

"Oh yeah." She shoots me a look I can't decipher then throws open her door.

I open mine and get out, too. I don't plan to go in, but I'd be a dick not to make sure she gets into her apartment safely. She's still wasted.

I escort her upstairs and take her keys from her to open the door. "*Spokoynoy nochi,*" I say.

"What's that mean?"

"Good night."

She stops and turns then surprises me by reaching out and fisting my shirt. She gives a tug.

63

At first I don't move, but as much as I don't want to take advantage of her right now, I also don't want to leave.

She's far too enthralling.

"You should come inside." Her words tumble out, one right on the top of the other.

"I'm inside," I concede, letting her pull me in and shut the door.

She takes her jacket off and throws it on a hook. Then strips me of mine.

"I'm not having sex with you, *zayka*."

She untucks my shirt from my pants and slides her hands beneath it, her palms making contact with my skin. A breath shudders in as she strokes over my abs. "You're not?" She's not pouting. It's more confusion in her expression.

"No, Freckles. You've had too much to drink. I'm not going to take advantage."

"Please? I do need sex. Shanna was right about that. And even though I don't usually do players, I think this one time might help me get it out of my system. Just this once, you know?"

My resolve firms. I'm definitely not going to be her "just this once" guy.

Still, my dick is hard because her hands keep stroking up inside my shirt. I chuckle and catch her hand when she pinches my nipple. "You're making it very hard to be a gentleman."

"Screw gentleman. I need some action. Please? What about that spanking you wanted to give me?"

I laugh because I knew that threat had tweaked her. "You need a spanking, Chelle?" I tug her hands out of my shirt and pin them behind her back. Her face lights up as I walk her backward toward her couch.

"Hmm? Answer me, little bunny. You want me to smack that cute ass of yours?"

"Um, kind of," she admits. Her face is flushed, but her eyes dance with pleasure.

I sit on the sofa and tug her over my lap with her torso on the sofa, her legs extended toward the floor. I give her ass one smack to see how she reacts.

She squeals and kicks her legs then wiggles her ass for more. She's in a pencil skirt like she'd gone to the lounge straight from work, and I tug it up. My cock surges when I see what's underneath. Not full pantyhose, but the thigh-high kind with the lace around the top that looks like garters. The hose are black, and so are her panties. Her black kitten heels complete the art-porn look.

"Aw, *zayka*, you look so hot in these." I palm her ass and squeeze and she rolls her hips over my lap. I give her ass another hard slap, and she jerks, then rolls her hips again. "You have the cutest ass I have ever had the pleasure of spanking."

I lightly stroke my fingers between her legs over her panties, and she humps my lap.

"Okay, ready for your spanking?"

She looks over her shoulder quizzically, and I give her a smirk as I gather her wrists at her lower back with one hand and start spanking her in earnest with the other.

"Eek!" She kicks her pretty shoes, and I clamp my leg down over hers to hold them still.

"You asked for it," I remind her as I continue to spank with a steady beat, warming her ass all over.

She makes the most adorable noises—squeaks and ohs and ahs that make me want to put her on her hands and knees and plow into her until we both see stars.

But I won't.

Not tonight, anyway.

Which means I'm going to take out my lust on her sexy, squirming ass. I continue to paddle her until her cries sound breathless, and she starts gasping my name.

I stop and release her legs, so I can pull down her satin panties.

She rolls her hips again. "No more," she whimpers.

I stroke between her legs. "No more, bunny rabbit? How about this? You want more of this?"

"Yes, oh please," she cries, her hips bucking from my touch.

I find her clit and swipe over it before I slide down to her entrance to gather her juices.

"Oh my *gawd*." She sounds shocked in a good way, which I love.

I rub more firmly, circling up to her clit, then screwing my index finger into her tight entrance. She squeezes around my finger which makes my dick press furiously against my zipper.

I release her wrists in favor of using the thumb of my other hand to explore the cleft between her reddened cheeks. When I find the tight button of her anus, she squeezes her ass together. I give her a light spank. "You want me to take care of this ache, Chelle?" I stroke over her clit with a slow, steady motion.

"Yes," she wails.

"Then be a good girl and let me finger-fuck your ass, too. It will make it so much better, I promise."

She goes still, like she's listening intently, or maybe she was thinking because after a moment she parts her legs further and relaxes the muscles of her ass.

I drop a little spit between her cheeks to use as lubricant and press my thumb against her asshole until she relaxes it and yields. As soon as I'm in, I reward her with swift, plunging strokes into her pussy, using two fingers face down, so I can rub over her G-spot.

She chokes on a cry, lifting one foot in a pretty pose. "Oh! Nikolai!" she cries out.

I wiggle my thumb inside her ass as I continue to finger-fuck her tight channel.

"Oh my God, this is so crazy! I can't...I need... oh!"

She comes, her anus and pussy squeezing around my digits in beautiful pulsing waves.

I wait until they finish, then give a few more slow pumps to milk out the aftershocks.

"Ohhhh," she moans.

I ease my fingers out and lean down to kiss her pink buttcheek. "Did you like your spanking?"

"Oh my God," she pants.

"Is that a *yes*?" I pull up her panties and unzip her skirt so it falls down when I help her to stand.

Her golden eyes are unfocused, and her chestnut waves are a messy halo around her flushed face. She nods but seems incapable of speech.

I'm absurdly pleased with myself for having done this to her.

"Let's get you to bed." It's only nine, but she could probably crash now and sleep it off. I stand from the couch and give her cute ass another smack. "Go brush your teeth, and I'll get you a glass of water. You definitely should rehydrate."

"Mmm."

I wash my hands in the kitchen, then get a glass of water and find ibuprofen in one of the cabinets. When I return, she's already belly flopped on her bed. I help her under the covers and set the water and ibuprofen beside her.

"Goodnight, little bunny." I drop a kiss on her forehead before I turn out the light and shut her bedroom door.

In the kitchen, I use a notepad and pen to scribble a message before I leave.

As I walk out, the image of her rumpled and satisfied stays in front of my eyes. I should banish it, but I don't.

It's an image I won't soon forget.

Especially because I doubt I'll be seeing it again. I may not have fucked Chelle, but I still went too far. I shouldn't have taken any liberties with her. Not when I know with total certainty that she will regret everything we did in the morning.

I won't get a redo of tonight. Not unless I get her drunk again, which I would never do.

I need to forget this woman because even though we share an attraction, she's not ever going to get over her prejudice toward me.

I'm the guy who beat up her brother.

I'm in the bratva.

And a player, according to her.

A woman like Chelle would never lower her standards to date a thug like me.

6

Chelle

Oh God. My head.

My alarm goes off way too early, sending shock waves through my system that makes me sit up with a gasp.

I see a glass of water and ibuprofen on my bedside table, and it all comes rushing back.

The guy buying me too many drinks at the lounge.

Nikolai showing up to rescue me. Wait… how did that happen? It seems like far too much of a coincidence, doesn't it?

"Oh God," I mutter when I remember the glorious horrible remainder of the night. I reach back and grab my ass on the way to the shower.

It's a little sore, but in a good way. What we did—well, what he did because I was more of a recipient than a participant—was off the charts hot. I've never done anything remotely kinky before in my life, and now that I've experienced it, I'm pretty sure it's my thing.

But—oh my God—with Nikolai? What in the world was I thinking? He's a thug and a player. I'm so embarrassed. My brain rewinds, trying to remember all the things I said last night. How much I revealed. I remember I called him a player. Did I really beg him to spank me?

Cringe, cringe, cringe!

He's worse than a perfect stranger plucked from a bar. He's Russian *mafiya*. A gangster my brother owes thirty grand to. What if last night was him showing me—and Zane—just how much he's in charge?

But no, that didn't fit. He was respectful. He refused to have sex with me, even though I was begging for it. And he left the glass of water and ibuprofen.

I try to ignore the warm flutters in my chest the memories produce. I'm not going to become enamored with this guy. A bigger mistake couldn't be made.

I shower and quickly get dressed for work. In the kitchen, I tell my Echo to play a morning acoustical mix and pull a yogurt out of the refrigerator. I eat it at the same time I make myself a mug of hot tea, then sit and check emails from work on my phone as I sip it.

Singing along to the song playing, I get up to wash my spoon and mug. That's when I see the note. My stomach flip flops.

Printed in crisp boxy letters, a message is centered in the middle of the paper.

Chelle Goldberg, you are adorable. Think of me when you sit today. —N

Underneath it is a neatly-printed phone number.

My face flushes as I snatch the note up. I crumple it, needing to destroy any evidence of my out-of-character behavior last night. But when I cock my hand to toss it in the trash, something stops it.

No.

I shouldn't keep his number.

But what if I need it? Like, for Zane, not for me. I

wouldn't keep it for me. I definitely would never call him for a repeat of what we did last night.

I smooth the note and take a picture of it with my phone. There. Now I can throw it away. I toss it in the trash and finish getting ready for work.

And then because I'm crazy, I go back and snatch the damn note out of the trash again and shove it in my purse.

～

Nikolai

I sit back in my chair, fold my arms over my chest, and smirk.

Dima hacked the feed through Chelle's Echo device, so I can watch her in her kitchen. It's a total violation of her privacy, but I don't give a shit.

Dima's complete cyberstalker package told me Chelle keeps a pretty structured and predictable schedule. Work. Workouts at a spin gym four days a week, the Wednesday hump day happy hour, and little else. Now that I've determined there isn't a man she meets at the Red Room, I can decide what to do with my newfound interest.

And no, I don't feel the slightest bit guilty over spying on her. My twin brother spies on anyone and everyone he pleases, so to me it feels more like a right than a crime. Besides, it was so worth it to watch her reaction to my note.

As I expected, she's embarrassed. I saw the flush of her face when she read it and how quick she was to crumple it up. But she saved it.

I don't know whether she'll call.

I'm not even sure I want her to. I'm looking for something real, and she's not someone who could ever accept who and what I am into her life. I'm sure most of my appeal is the dangerous bad boy thing.

Then again, I wouldn't have said Ravil had a chance in hell of convincing Lucy, the city's top defense attorney, into staying with him, but she has. Of course, he didn't give her much of a choice.

The idea of bending Chelle to my will that same way has an appeal. She'd do anything to save her brother, I know that.

But I've spent my entire adult life using pressure points or violence to bend people to my will. I don't want that in the bedroom too.

My phone buzzes with a text from Ravil, so I shut down my laptop and get my ass upstairs to heed his summons.

All the inner circle is in his office—Oleg, Maxim, Adrian, me. Dima's on video-conference.

Ravil sits back and laces his hands behind his head. "Lucy just turned down representing a member of a motorcycle club called Devil Dawgs. He was brought in on drug charges, but the police were investigating him for suspected human trafficking as well."

Adrian's body jerks, and his upper lip curls.

I know Ravil's only making this his business because otherwise Adrian will involve himself on his own, and get himself in trouble again. He nearly went to trial last year for arson when he burned Leon Poval's factory to the ground in retaliation for what was done to his sister.

"They're led by someone who goes by the name of Viper. There's no clear connection to Poval, but I think we should find out for sure, no?"

"Did Lucy give you the name of her would-be client? I can research that way," Dima offers.

"I'll get it for you. But I want you guys to get out there and ask around."

"They will think we want in on it," Maxim warns.

"Let them," Ravil says. "I don't mind an excuse to step on cockroaches."

Maxim nods. "All right. We go in pairs. Nikolai with Oleg. I'll go with Adrian. Ask to make a small score to get your foot in the door."

"Good," Ravil nods. "Report back with anything you find."

Oleg and I file out and pick up weapons and cash before we take the elevator to the parking lot.

I don't mind the assignment. It's dangerous but Oleg and I can hold our own. When Dima and I first joined the bratva, if our *pakhan* gave an order, we scrambled to comply just to keep our own throats from being slit.

After being placed under Ravil, we functioned more out of an urge to please our boss. Whatever he asked, we delivered with the intention of impressing him.

I turned being the bratva's bookie into a life purpose. Running the poker games is a pleasure for me. I like my role as host. I don't mind the blood and violence of calling in my markers.

I love handling the money. In addition to the poker games, I run sports bets and general loan shark shit.

Ravil also gives microloans to Russian tenants in his building. Start-up loans for their businesses, shit like that. If they default, I don't bust noses and break fingers. Maxim, Ravil and I go in to look at their businesses and make changes to bring them to profit. Do they have a choice in those changes? Fuck, no. We still own them. But we don't use violence.

Does anyone try to screw Ravil over?

No. No one has yet, anyway. Everyone is usually so fucking grateful they would name their first born children after him.

This shit on the street isn't my favorite thing. In the

past, the danger and need to please Ravil would be enough to keep me from complaining, but the farther removed from the street we get, the less appeal it holds. Today, going out to score drugs and get info on sex-trafficking feels like a kick in the nuts.

It has something to do with Chelle Goldberg although I'm not sure what. I already knew she wouldn't hang with a guy like me, even if she only knew my very best parts.

I guess this work feels like a confirmation of what she already believes about me, even though we're only doing it as detective work to find Leon Poval. She thinks I'm a thug who has badly influenced her brother. Buying drugs on the street wouldn't look good to her. It would confirm her belief that I'm not anyone whose life should dissect hers.

Oleg and I make a few visits before I get the name of a dealer who goes by Rattlesnake. I figure one snake name probably follows another. We meet him behind a gas station convenience store. He's dressed in a leather vest and has a long, untrimmed beard. I'm guessing his organization is a motorcycle club. It's obviously a very classy operation.

"I heard you work for Viper," I drop casually as I hand over fifteen hundred dollars for twenty grams of coke. It's a waste of money because I will flush the shit. Ravil doesn't allow any drugs into the Kremlin, not that I ever had a taste for it.

The guy has snake tattoos crawling up his neck onto the side of his face. He stares at me for a minute with a completely blank face then casually reaches for his pistol.

I force myself not to flinch. I've never had a death wish. Not like Dima in his reckless years when he wanted to die. But I don't waste energy on fear either.

After getting shot this past summer though, it's hard not to remember the fragility of this body. But I also learned its resilience. I know there's no way Oleg will let me get shot again because he blamed himself for what went down last time. He's close enough to this *mudak* that he could disarm and shoot him in the head before the guy could blink.

"You a cop?" the guy asks, pointing the gun at my head. His question significantly lowers my opinion of him. If that's all he's worried about, he has no idea how dangerous I really am to him and his organization.

"Not a cop," I say smoothly. "I'm interested in some of your boss' business dealings. I'd like to buy his other product."

Rattlesnake looks at me unblinkingly for another minute, and I wonder if that's where he gets his nickname. His stare *is* very snakelike. "Who are you?" he says at last.

"Nikolai Novikov."

"You Russian?"

"Obviously."

"Russian *mafiya*?"

I incline my head.

He splits a look between Oleg and me then puts his pistol away. "You want pussy?"

"We want to purchase. Not rent." I keep the disgust from showing on my face.

"How many?"

I shrug my shoulders. "As many as you're willing to part with."

"You got a number?"

I pull out a card and hand it to him. It's a simple one with just my name and a VPN number Dima set up that can't be traced. My last name isn't real either. I picked it when we joined the bratva and had to create new identities. I liked the ring of Novikov with my first name.

Dima thinks it's utterly ridiculous to have business

cards in this day and age with cell phones and digital data, but there's a part of my job that involves schmoozing. I have to get people to bet with me and to come back again and again. Having a card to hand out comes in handy sometimes.

Rattlesnake takes my card and pockets it. "I'll give it to the boss. I don't know if he's selling, but he might be."

"Is he the...original owner?"

Rattlesnake pushes his lower lip out and shakes his head. "Nah. Some guy offloaded them a few months back. He dumped them real cheap, but they're a pain in the ass."

"American?"

Rattlesnake narrows his eyes. "Why do you ask?"

My skin prickles. If he was American, seems like Rattlesnake would've just said. Poval is Ukrainian. The slave owner could've been one of his men who stayed behind after Adrian torched the sofa factory and Poval disappeared.

"Just curious. I appreciate the connection. And the blow." I hold up the bag of cocaine.

He gives me that weird unblinking stare again and then nods. "*Do svidaniya*." He lifts his hand in a wave as he walks away.

A chill runs through me. Maybe he knows Russian because that's where the sex slaves are from. Maybe this really is a link to Leon Poval and his flesh trade of Russian girls like Nadia, Adrian's sister.

I don't know if Ravil will tell Adrian what we've found out or not. He has the tendency to fly solo, and while he's learned a lot from us in the year he's been with the cell, he's still young. He got himself caught when he torched Leon's sofa factory after finding and rescuing his sister from its depths.

Oleg waits until Rattlesnake has walked away before he makes a ferocious-sounding growl in his throat.

"Agreed," I mutter. "I think we may have found the trail to Poval. Hold off telling Adrian until the *pakhan* gives us instruction."

Oleg frowns and signs, *I don't talk.*

"Well, you talk more than you used to." I slap him on the back.

~

Nikolai

A day later, Oleg, Adrian and I catch Zane outside one of his classes. Yes, I have his complete class schedule because obtaining it was easy work for Dima.

The minute he sees us he starts to run in the opposite direction.

"Don't make me chase you." I don't even raise my voice.

Zane slows and then stops, keeping his back to me. We flank him, Oleg dropping a meaty hand on his shoulder.

"Take him to the parking garage," I say in Russian to keep Zane in the dark.

Oleg maneuvers Zane to a corner in the high-rise concrete garage where he turns him around to face me.

"You know why I'm here?"

Zane pales, his skin turning green around his mouth like he's going to puke. His shoulders sag. "The ring."

"*Da.* The ring."

"I'll get you another payment."

"I know you will," I say smoothly. "This visit isn't about what you owe." I punch him in the nose, hearing the snap as it folds to the side.

He doubles over, clutching it.

"That was for sending your sister to my place." Blood starts to pour onto his shoes. Oleg lifts his torso with a single hand on his shoulder. I punch him in the gut. "And that was for making her cry."

He staggers backward into Oleg. I nod to Oleg to straighten him again, and when he does, I step up close. He flinches when I reach for his face and place my thumbs on either side of his nose. With another snap, I straighten the break.

"Do better, *mudak*. Your sister doesn't deserve to carry your shit."

Zane splutters and opens his mouth like he's going to backtalk, but when I raise my brows, he closes it again.

I tip my head, which Oleg correctly deciphers to mean, *release him*.

"See you Friday," I say as we walk away.

I think I hear Zane mutter *fuck you* as we leave, but I let it slide.

7

Chelle

Janette's been in the conference room with the potential clients—the skateboarding stars from the group Skate 32—all afternoon.

I thought they'd be younger for some reason. I guess because she described them that way. But they're more of that Peter Pan, *won't grow up,* type. Like pushing thirty but still dressing and acting like they're sixteen. I saw no signs of professionalism or business-sense from them when I brought in drinks and snacks.

But I guess that's why they need us.

It's close to five when Janette shows up at my desk. She appears pale and sweaty, which makes me stand to meet her, worried something has gone wrong.

"Oh my God, I think I ate something bad for lunch," she says. "I just puked my guts out in the bathroom—sorry for the TMI. Listen, I need to get home. I can't take these guys out tonight."

"Oh, I'm sure they'll understand," I say quickly. "I will let them know you had to cancel."

"No," she says sharply, clearly annoyed with me. "We need to get them signed. You have to take them out. Show them the town—use that list you made me."

"Oh, uh…yeah. Okay."

"But bring a date. These guys seem a little randy. I don't feel comfortable sending you out with them alone."

A date? I look around the office wildly, but as usual, I'm the only one still here on a Friday night.

"Bring a guy. Say he's your boyfriend. I mean, I don't think they're dangerous, but I don't want things to be awkward for you, okay?"

Yipes. Maybe Zane will go with me. Or would they know he's not a boyfriend because we look too much alike?

She clutches her stomach. "Oh God, I've got to go. Let them know you'll pick them up at their hotel in an hour or two. Is your car clean? Take a cab if it's not." She groans. "I really have to go. You close this deal, and I'll make you a Junior Publicist."

Wow. Okay. That's an offer I can't turn down.

"I will close the deal," I promise, even though I have maybe twenty percent confidence in my ability to do so. I mean, she didn't even invite me in the conference room with them today, and I'm the one who put the presentation together.

This could be my chance to prove myself. Finally become a publicist instead of the damn assistant.

I square my shoulders and march into the conference room. "Hey, guys."

"The assistant!" One of them calls out like he's excited to see me. "What are we still doing here, Assistant? I thought you were taking us out."

"Ooh, she's our date for the night? Not bad. Better than Pant-suit." He jerks his thumb toward the door. I don't think Janette would mind the moniker.

Doggy-farts. I definitely need a date tonight.

I try not to think of that crumpled note in my purse. I have absolutely no plans to call Nikolai. Ever. I mean, never, ever.

"Janette said you'd take us wherever we want to go on the company dime, so I'm thinking we want the most expensive sushi restaurant in the city. Can you hook us up, Assistant?"

"Um…" My mind races, not just trying to figure out which restaurant to take them to but also reeling from the complete understanding of how ill-equipped I am to handle these guys.

They are definitely rowdy. Totally disrespectful.

I can see why Janette thought I needed a chaperone. But I can't go full-bitch mode—my usual go-to when my back is up against a wall—because I'm supposed to close this deal.

I draw myself up. "My name is Chelle, call me Chelle," I say firmly. "What are your names?"

"Tiny," the short one says, holding up his hand.

"Randy," another one says, making the word sound suggestive.

"Is that your name or an adjective?"

He grins because I got his joke. "Both."

"Great. And you?" I raise my brows at the third guy.

"Bones," he answers.

"Bones." I bite back any commentary I might have on their names.

"Okay, Tiny, Randy, and Bones. I can definitely take you for good sushi, but Janette had reservations at an upscale Mexican restaurant. It's very popular—"

"Nope," Bones interrupts. "We want sushi."

"*Expensive* sushi," Tiny chimes in.

I manage not to roll my eyes. "Okay, I'll see if I can get

us a reservation. You guys can head back to your hotel to get ready for dinner, and I'll pick you up at seven."

"I don't need to get ready," Randy says.

"We don't have to dress up or anything, do we?" Tiny complains.

"*I* need to get ready," I say firmly. "Give me your cell, and I'll call you when I get to your hotel."

Randy gives me his number, and I manage to get the guys out, then collapse into my desk chair and groan. I try to get reservations at the three best sushi restaurants and strike out with all three. It's a Friday night. Not even throwing around our firm's name does any good.

Crap on a cracker. I don't have a date or a place to go.

I draw a measured breath and pull the crumpled note from Nikolai from my purse. It's a bad idea. The worst, really.

Things could go very wrong, and these are potential clients I need to convince to sign with us. But I'm really not sure I can handle them on my own.

I flatten the note on my desk and pick up my phone. *Here goes the worst plan ever.*

I dial Nikolai's number. He picks up on the second ring.

"I did not expect you to call."

"Um, I didn't expect me to call either. I'm not calling for—um. Yeah. I'm not calling for that. What we did last night. I need a huge, huge favor."

"You're calling me for a favor?" He sounds surprised. I knew this was a bad idea. "I believe you already owe me one for giving you that ring back."

"I know. I totally know. I just… *ack.*"

"What is it?" His voice sharpens a little like he thinks I'm in danger or something.

"My boss got sick, and I'm supposed to take these guys

out tonight and show them a good time and convince them to sign with us, but they're a little rowdy, and I sort of need a fake boyfriend again."

"How many rowdy guys?"

"Three. They're skateboarders. And they want the best sushi in town, but I don't have a reservation anywhere, so I have to figure something out."

"Okay. I'll be your bodyguard. What time?"

Unexpected relief sweeps through me. "You'll do it?"

"What time, Chelle?"

"I'm supposed to pick them up by seven at the Hotel Grand. I have to—"

"I'll pick you up at 6:35," he cuts in.

"Oh. You will? Do you have room for all of us in your Tesla?"

"I'll bring an SUV."

"Um—"

"Bye, Chelle." He ends the call before I can say anything else.

I try to ignore the way my insides seem to pop and fizz with excitement that he's coming as my date. Or pleasure at the way he says my name.

Chelle Goldberg, you are adorable. I remember the words before my eyes seek the proof of them on the note.

It's okay that I called him.

It's just for work.

Only because I was in a pickle and had no other choice.

Nikolai

I text Chelle when I'm outside her apartment, and she comes jogging out in another pencil skirt and knee-high boots. She climbs in the front seat smelling of some honey-warm scent that makes me want to lick every inch of her.

"I like the boots."

"I like the jacket," she says, noting the black suit jacket I wore over my lavender button down. When you have as many tats as I do, you have to dress up a little to be taken seriously. I learned that art from Ravil and Maxim who always look like they're stepping off the cover of a men's magazine.

Electricity zings between us—a low-level excitement like we're on a real date and not some strange work-related favor.

"Thank you for doing this." She sounds a little breathless.

"There will be a price," I tell her, letting my lips kick up, so she doesn't totally freak out. I don't mind her being a little on edge with me.

She should be. The truth is, I am dangerous. I operate using the theater of fear, so making people think I'm safe would be a mistake. Her brother owes me a ton of money, and I can't let him off the hook for it.

She looks down and rummages in her purse and pulls out her phone. "I need to get us a reservation somewhere," she says. "Ideas? They wanted high-end sushi."

"They're just throwing their weight around to see how willing you are to cater to their demands. Do they think they're rock stars?"

"Clearly."

"Let's go to Lucky Roll." I name the most expensive sushi place I've heard of. Plates start at three hundred bucks. I only know of it because Maxim and Sasha are fans and have brought us out before.

"I already tried there. They said they don't have reservations open on a weekend for months."

"I can get us in," I say, with only half-confidence it's true. I saw Maxim grease the maitre d's palm to get us in last time. It might work again tonight. It's worth a try. Of course, if I fail, it could be awkward.

I drive to the hotel, and she texts her would-be clients to come down.

The moment I see them, I relax a bit. I can handle these assholes, no problem. Now I understand why she called me and not someone else.

They are from the street like me.

I get out of the SUV for introductions and Chelle follows my lead.

"Nikolai, this is Bones, Tiny, and Randy. Guys, this is my boyfriend, Nikolai."

They take in my tats and seem to approve, each giving me some slapping fist-bumping kind of handshake that I roll with.

"Niko!" Bones says. "Can I call you Niko?"

"No you may not," I answer immediately.

"Oh, schwang!" Tiny chortles—whatever that means —as Randy makes a gong sound.

I herd the guys into the backseat of the SUV and drive to Lucky Roll.

"So I heard you're big porn stars," I say with a straight face.

"What?" Tiny asks

"Hell, yeah." Bones grins. "Where do you think I got my name?"

Chelle groans loudly while the guys in the back chuckle.

"No, really. What is it you do? You're skateboarders?"

"Yep. Youtubers. We have a channel with twenty million followers," Randy says.

I whistle. "Impressive. So why do you need a publicist?" I glance in the rearview mirror as I drive.

"Yeah, I don't think we do," Bones asserts, folding his arms over his chest.

Randy just smirks.

Tiny shrugs. "We have an online store that we want to expand. Maybe franchise. We need branding and shit."

I nod. "Cool."

Chelle pivots in her seat. "What did you think about what Janette presented today?"

I check their faces in the rearview mirror. None of them seem that impressed, but I also get the sense they're playing Chelle. Milking her for the expensive dinner and entertainment while they make up their minds.

I find a parking place in the underground lot beneath the restaurant, and we take the elevator up to the top floor. The restaurant appears packed. "Give me a minute," I say to Chelle and walk over to the host station. I pull out a wad of hundred dollar bills and peel four off the top to hold between my fingers.

I show the money to the maitre d. "Listen, my girlfriend has these VIPs in town, and they insisted on your restaurant for dinner." The guys aren't dressed appropriately for a nice restaurant, which is part of why I called them VIPs. Hopefully their presumed celebrity status will give them a pass on their appearance. "I know you're packed, but is there any way you could find us a table for five?"

The guy looks down at the money and then back at me. "Certainly, sir." He smoothly takes the bills from me. "I have a private table for you with the best view of the city. Give me just a few minutes to put it together."

I nod and he disappears.

When I walk back, Chelle's golden eyes are locked on my face with a sort of startled expectation.

I give her a nod and watch her small frame relax a bit.

Taking care of her feels good. I suddenly wish I was here alone with Chelle. On a real date. Considering I never go on dates, it's a strange desire. But I also never stalk women, and I've got Chelle firmly in my sights now.

The host returns and escorts us to the table, and the guys proceed to order the most expensive drinks and sushi on the menu. Chelle wisely chooses to stick with water.

I make conversation by asking questions and keeping them engaged. The kind of shit I do every Friday night at the games. The liquor makes them rowdier, but they're not unmanageable.

"So what do you do, Nikolai?" Randy asks.

I meet his gaze steadily. "I am Russian *mafiya*."

~

CHELLE

I choke on my water.

The guys laugh, then Tiny says, "I can't tell if he's serious."

"Of course he's not," I interject. "He's an accountant."

"*Da*," Nikolai agrees. "I run numbers."

I make a huge show of rolling my eyes like he's kidding. All the while, my stomach is stuck up in my solar plexus.

This dinner is going to cost a literal fortune—I've been adding things up in my head, and we've already easily passed two grand. That's not even counting the money Nikolai paid to get us a table. I'm sure I'll be paying that back with a ton of interest, too. I have the company credit card, but if I don't land this deal, Janette will probably kill me.

I couldn't be more stressed out.

The only thing that's gone right about tonight is, well, Nikolai.

He's my saving grace. He got us into this place. He somehow has control of my raucous guests, and I actually think they like him.

I can't imagine how awkward and different tonight would be without him.

To make matters worse, the guys keep ordering more drinks and more sushi. I swear they challenged each other to rack up the highest bill possible.

Actually, I wouldn't be surprised if that's exactly their plan. They're probably secretly filming this to put on their Youtube channel and make fun of me. I look for hidden cameras, but don't see any. Then again, what do I know about that sort of thing?

When the bill finally comes, I refuse to look at it. I just pull out the American Express and put it in the folder.

"Thank you for dinner," Boner says with a mischievous look.

Yep, they were definitely working me.

"Now we'd like to see Chicago's nightlife. Janette was promising to take us out on the town."

"Sure, we could go—"

"Take us to a strip club!" Randy interrupts.

"Hey," Nikolai says sharply, making all three of them look. "That's my girlfriend you're talking to, so show a little respect, or I'll shove your head in the toilet back there. What do Americans call that? A swirly?"

The other two guys make "ooh" noises. "Oh, I think he would, too," Tiny says.

Randy looks at me. "Is he really in the Russian *mafiya*?"

"We don't discuss that," I say primly, finally playing along like it's all a big joke.

Nikolai shoots me a satisfied smile and pushes back his chair to stand. "My friend's band is playing not far from here. Come on, you'll like them."

The guys all follow like Nikolai's their natural leader.

It takes me a minute to reorient. I had my list of possible things to do running in my head, and my mind was still spinning trying to pick the best when I realize I'm off the hook. Nikolai has this evening in hand.

Thank God for my unlikely hero.

But no, Nikolai isn't a hero. I have to remind myself. He's a dangerous felon. He probably kills people in back alleys. He definitely uses violence and extortion to get his way. And worst of all, he's got my brother's balls in a vise right now. Characterizing him as a hero would be a mistake of epic proportions.

Still, I can't find it in me to regret asking him to handle tonight.

I'll probably regret it plenty when he calls in his favor.

Hopefully it won't be anything illegal or unsavory. I can't decide if I hope or don't hope it will be sexual in nature.

I can't think about that now. I just have to get through tonight.

NIKOLAI TAKES us to a grungy sort of pub. It's nothing I would ever pick to take a potential client to, but the guys from Skate 32 seem to love it.

There's a band on the stage, but they're not playing. They're tuning and getting set up still.

"Nikolai!" A young woman with a Debbie Harry platinum-blonde bob waves from the stage, and something in me turns brittle and hard.

Ugh. Of course his friend with a band is female.

Nikolai is a total player. That's why he's so good at handling this random weird social event. He's the kind of guy who takes out a different girl every weekend. Totally practiced at this sort of thing.

Nikolai finds us a table toward the back corner because he says it's going to get loud. I position my chair on the end, as far removed from all of them as I can manage. I'm out of energy for all of this. I definitely can't handle any of these guys, including the one I voluntarily invited along.

Nikolai leans forward and hooks a hand under the seat of my chair to drag me around the corner beside him.

I shriek a little when it tips, and he slows down but keeps pulling until I'm right beside him. "I won't let you fall," he says, like I should know that already.

A cocktail waitress comes to take our order, and she knows Nikolai's name, too.

I can't stop the burn of jealousy that coats my mouth and throat.

Nikolai eyes me. "Are you doing okay?"

"I'm fine," I lie. I will be as soon as I get through this night. But then I can't stop myself. "So you're friends with the band?"

He nods. "With Story." He lifts his chin toward the blonde.

I want to leave. Maybe I could go? Would that be too weird? The band probably sucks.

No, that's absurd. I can't leave. I'm supposed to ensure this deal gets closed by tomorrow.

I swallow down the bile in my throat. "Are you guys, like…"

Nikolai scoffs softly with an amused smile. "Story and I?" He gestures between them. "No. Just wait a minute, and it will all become clear."

I frown, hating the mystery. What will become clear?

"Watch." He tips his head toward a group coming in the door. I can't figure out what he's talking about. The group settles in at tables right in front of the stage. And then he's right. It becomes infinitely clear.

Because Story takes a running leap off the stage and lands squarely in the arms of an enormous, tattooed man.

A guy I recognize from the hotel suite where they had their poker game.

Everything hard and pointy inside me suddenly melts into warm caramel. The public display of affection is adorable. To see the way the muscled giant stares up at his girlfriend with total love makes me swoon.

"She's your *friend's* girlfriend," I say with relief.

Nikolai's smile is warm, but his gaze isn't on them, it's on me. "*Da*. They are my roommates. All of them."

It's weird.

A squishy, uncomfortable but warm weird.

Because in this moment, Nikolai suddenly becomes human to me.

He isn't just the bratva bookie. The monster who loans money and beats faces in to get it paid back.

He's a guy with roommates and friends.

Friends who obviously love deeply.

I watch the big guy carry Story back to the stage and gently lift her onto it. She picks up her electric guitar, nods at her bandmates, and they launch into a fun, fast-paced song.

The skaters, who were busy slamming a round of vodka shots Nikolai ordered, cheer, apparently loving the music.

Nikolai tosses a long arm around the back of my chair, casually claiming me, as if we are on a real date. Are a real couple. I like the way it feels. For a minute, I pretend this is actually my life. I'm here with Nikolai and his friends, enjoying live music.

"Do they play here a lot?" I ask, trying to get a larger glimpse into his life.

He nods. "Every Thursday. Do you like it?"

"Yeah. They're good. Totally."

"Welcome, everyone!" the lead singer says into the mic. "I'm Story, and we're the Storytellers." She peers back in our direction. "I hear we have some special guests tonight. Nikolai, did you bring the guys from Skate 32?"

Boner, Tiny and Randy go nuts, surging to their feet and whooping and hollering like their team just scored a goal.

"My brother, Flynn, is a big fan." She jerks her thumb behind her toward the lead guitarist who looks like a younger version of her.

Flynn gives them a hang loose sign with his tongue out.

I can't believe it.

"Did you know?" I ask Nikolai, who laughs and shakes his head in equal disbelief.

After that, the party is on. I forget to monitor my guests because they're having a great time. Conversation gets more relaxed, their boisterousness is less combative, taking on a more celebratory vibe.

Halfway through the second set, Nikolai pulls me onto his lap.

"Stop, what are you doing?" I demand, trying not to make a scene as I attempt to wiggle back to my chair.

"Shh. You're my girlfriend. Act like it."

"Nikolai…"

"Hush." He uses the arm around my waist to drag me higher over his lap. "Watch the band."

I sit stiffly for a few minutes, then start to relax as he traces light circles around my knee with his fingertips. I shouldn't be sitting on Nikolai's lap. Even if he was my legit boyfriend—which he absolutely is not—it would be unprofessional. I'm here with potential clients. Then again, said clients are getting sloshed and watching the band, not me. There's also the fact that Nikolai's fingers start trailing up my inner thigh, and it's making my pulse race. Especially because I vaguely remember—all right, I remember in perfect detail—how skilled he is with his fingers. Especially in the region of my body where he's headed.

I squirm a little on his lap, my mind taking a spin around the "this is a horrible idea" track again while his fingers send tingles up and down my spine.

Nikolai's teeth score my shoulder, and I grind right down on his lap, losing my breath. "Were you sore today, Freckles?" His hot breath is at my nape.

I both shake and nod my head at the same time.

"Were you mad?"

It's a funny question considering I'm the one who begged him for it last night, but I appreciate it. It did hurt a bit, and I was drunk. His question shows a level of consideration I wouldn't expect from a guy like him.

Except I'm starting to realize I don't know what a *guy like him* actually is. I had a fuzzy stereotype cobbled together from the movies and based on what he did to Zane. But other parts don't really fit.

His fingers slide up my skirt, just lightly skimming over my hose. "I like your tight skirts, *zayka*. You dress like you're going to be boss bitch some day soon."

I twist to see his face because the words surprise me. They also satisfy and fluster me. Like this guy sees me in a skirt two days in a row and suddenly knows my life goals or something.

His blue gaze is on my face, intent and more serious than I expect.

"That's my plan," I say primly.

His lips quirk. "I'll stay out of your way, then." He winks, and I curse the way I cream my panties.

Player.

This guy is nothing but a player. That's why he's so damn good at seduction.

I can't let him be a repeat of Rob Sharke for me. I learned that lesson in the worst possible way a seventeen-year-old girl could.

Last night I had too much to drink. Tonight I'm sober. I should have better self-control. I should not be on this guy's lap.

But then he boldly cups my mons, and I let out a cry of pleasure. The sight alone of his hand disappearing under my rucked up skirt sends a bolt of hedonistic lust straight to my nether region. The black lace of my thigh-highs show, setting off the patch of pale skin sandwiched between the hose and the skirt. I snatch my jacket off the back of my chair and drape it over my lap, even though we're in the dark corner, and the table hides everything.

"I won't let anyone see," Nikolai promises in that scolding tone he used when he pulled the chair. Like I should know better than to doubt him.

He's moving his fingers over my panties now, and it's all I can do not to dance on his lap. He changes his angle with the arm around my waist to slide his hand up my sweater. When he pinches my nipple and rubs my clit at the same time, I jerk and cry out again.

Thankfully, the sound of my choked cry is drowned out by the boisterous sound filling the lounge.

I have to admit, the band is really cool. I'd pay more attention if—

Oh God.

Nikolai dips a finger inside me while maintaining pressure on my clit with his palm and rolling and tugging my nipple.

I want to laugh and cry at the same time. I'm too hot—needy and desperate, and I really want more than the tip of Nikolai's finger inside me.

I guess Shanna was right.

I really need to get laid

Otherwise, I wouldn't let this ridiculous, crazy thing happen right now.

I want to blame Nikolai—make him the devil—but he's not the one receiving pleasure.

I am.

He's doing all the giving.

"Why…" I squirm, trying to drive his finger deeper. He pushes a second one inside me.

"Why, what, Freckles? Why do I find you so hot? I'm not sure. I think it's something about that boss-bitch attitude in such a tiny package."

I buck my hips, coming around his fingers. I'm embarrassed and not quite satisfied. Also, more than a little confused by my helplessness to withstand Nikolai's charms.

He rubs my clit, and I come a little more, a full-body shudder running through me as I rest my head back on his shoulder and slump in his lap.

"Why are you doing this to me?" I croak, as if he just did something bad rather than something mind-blowing and fun. Something that was only for my pleasure and not for his.

"I didn't mean to," he murmurs back.

His words drape over my shoulders and settle there like a gossamer cape, woven of magic and mystery. Nikolai couldn't help himself either. This isn't something he's doing to me, but rather something we're in together.

8

Nikolai

As I drive the trio back to their hotel, I sense Chelle's stiffness return. She warmed up by the end of the show, not just to me, but to the guys and the band.

The Storytellers never put on a better show, and Chelle's skateboarding stars loved it. Whether it was the alcohol talking, or the fact that Flynn recognized them, and they felt famous, I couldn't be sure, but they mingled during the band's break, and by the time Rue's closed for the night, Chelle was brokering their drunken promises to use the Storyteller's music on their Youtube videos in some kind of collaboration

Guessing at her anxiety now that the night's almost over, I play ambassador.

"So are you guys going to sign on with Chelle and her boss, or were you just dicking her around tonight?"

A couple of the guys chuckle softly.

"No, we'll sign," Randy says easily. "I mean, we were dicking around, but yeah. Chelle, you're cool. You have my trust."

"Yeah, totally," Tiny agrees.

"Me too," Boner says.

"Thanks. That's great." Relief pours from Chelle. I see the first genuine smile on her face, and it's heart-stopping. "You'll come by tomorrow to sign the papers?"

"Yep. We'll be there. But we want to work with you not your stuffy boss, yeah?" Randy says.

"Okay." Chelle's smile is even bigger. "You might need to tell her that for me, okay?"

"Oh, we will," Randy swears.

I pull into the circle drive of their hotel and climb out to do their fist-bumping thing, but now they're all about man-hugs, slapping my back and breathing vodka in my face while they tell me what a great time they had.

When they go to give Chelle big hugs, I warn, "Grope my girlfriend, and I'll break all your fingers."

A chorus of good-natured whoa and whoos goes up, and they opt to shake her hand instead, which is good, because I wasn't fucking joking.

She may not be my girlfriend, but no one's going to get fresh with her on my watch.

In fact, I may have to appoint myself her permanent bodyguard if she's taking on these clowns as her personal clients.

"Thank you. You were great," Chelle says when we get back in the SUV.

I smile but don't answer. I like making her happy. I like making her come even more.

When I pull up to her place, I find a parking spot and turn off the engine.

Chelle goes rigid again. "You're not coming up with me because this wasn't a real date," she says.

I can't stand the idea of sex as a transaction, so I definitely wasn't thinking she owed me, but my dick has been hard ever since she ground that little ass over my lap and let me fuck her with my fingers, so I'm not quite ready to give up.

"Right, it wasn't a date, it was a favor." I put a suggestive note in my voice and twist to face her. Her hand is on the door handle, but she hasn't pulled it yet. "Hmm. I'll add it to what you owe me then." Remembering the price I exacted for the last favor I gave, I reach for her nape and tug her mouth to mine.

Her breath tastes like cinnamon mints, and her lips are as willing as her tight little body was back at Rue's. I kiss her slowly, savoring the softness of her mouth, the tentative movement of her tongue between my lips.

When I end it, her eyes are dilated. She still doesn't open the door. "Was that part of what I owe you?"

"No, that was me taking what I want," I admit.

"What do I owe you?"

"Oh, you'll know when I call it in." My voice sounds deeper than usual. I have to shift to rearrange my junk.

"You don't want to call it in tonight?" Her voice is husky.

I go still as my lust collides with the need to retain a little fucking pride.

I cock my head. "So it's okay for me to come up if it's a transaction but not if it's a date?"

She goes still. Her lips part, but she has no answer for that.

It's not entirely fair. She may have changed her mind because of the kiss, not because I'm not worthy, but I don't like feeling like my dick's in the wind here.

I tip my head toward the door. "Get out." I say it lightly to take away the sting.

She blinks. "What?"

"Get out, Chelle, we're done."

It still takes her a minute before she moves and when she does, there's dismay in her expression. Her golden eyes are round and sorry. "Okay," she says as she slides out of the seat and drops to the ground. "Um, bye."

I nod but don't answer. She swings the door shut then stops it halfway and puts her head back in. She opens her mouth. Shuts it again. "Yeah." She shuts the door.

I wait until I see she's safely in the building before I drive off. As I do, the finality of my words starts to crush me from the inside out. Did I mean it? That we're done?

Yeah, I guess I did.

There's no room for anything but sex. She wants the bad boy to get her off a few times without any structure of a relationship.

And for once in my life, I want something more. I deserve more.

After a lifetime of just trying to keep me and my twin alive, it's time to look beyond Friday night games and making money for the boss.

Everyone else has love.

Why can't I too?

My phone buzzes when I'm almost back at the Kremlin. I know without looking that it will be Chelle.

I feel like I offended you. I'm sorry. You were great tonight with the clients.

I don't answer.

I'm not a baby. It's not that I'm so offended or she hurt my feelings. I just realized it was time to cut bait. Chelle fascinates me, but it couldn't work.

I pull into the underground parking lot and park Oleg's SUV. On the elevator up to my floor, she texts again.

It's just that I don't know how to have sex with someone without marrying them in my mind.

I try not to warm up to her. This confess-all is cute, but it still doesn't mean—

Another text comes through. *I think I like the idea of sex as a transaction in the same way 1 in 5 women have fantasies of being forced. Or want to be tied up.*

Aw, fuck. Now I can't resist. *Do you want me to tie you up, Chelle?* I text back. The elevator doors slide open, and I step out, stopping in the empty hallway to wait for her reply.

What am I doing? I just decided at her place that I wanted more than sex, and it wasn't going to happen with her.

Um...yes? Maybe?

Why does she have to be so damn adorable? Everything she does is cute. I just can't get enough of it.

Before I can stop myself, I text, *Want to make a deal with the devil?*

My dick thickens at the wicked idea dancing around in my head. I ignore my hard-on and walk to my apartment.

I know it's against my rules. I know I wanted the real deal and not meaningless sex, but this is the opening she gave me. She doesn't want to date me. She wants sex as a transaction.

So, fuck it—she's worth breaking my rules for. I want her beneath me, writhing that tight little body of hers and moaning my name. I wouldn't mind a bit if she was tied up while I'm at it. Maybe she could wear my collar and a ball-gag. Call me *Daddy* or *Master* or *Sir.*

And I thought our bratva brother Pavel was the kinky one.

I use the keycard to open my door and walk inside. The place has never felt emptier. Leaving the lights off, I go straight to the bedroom and flop on my back.

Are you the devil? her message comes through.

RENEE ROSE

I snort as I text back, *Obviously.*

Maybe, she replies.

Yes or no?

Yes?

I shouldn't. Not because it's wrong but because sex is not a currency I accept. I mean, it's not like I can pay out my brothers their share. Well, I technically could, but I'd sooner cut my own balls off.

Fuck it.

30 nights and your brother's free.

As soon as I type it, I get hard as stone.

She texts back almost immediately. *Consecutive?*

Blyad', she's mine. My dick goes rock hard. I unzip my pants to let it out, but I don't let myself stroke it. The torture suddenly feels good. I could have Chelle's pouty lips stretched around my length by tomorrow night. I could turn her ass pink again and listen to her sweet little moans. Put her on her knees for me and teach her how to serve.

I am the devil, and I'm not even a little bit sorry for breaking my own rules.

Yes. I own you for one month, I text her. *You leave, you forfeit all.*

She doesn't answer for a moment, and I start to sweat. Maybe she'll tell me no. She's definitely thinking about it.

Do I get hard limits? It can't interfere with my job.

I almost fist pump in the darkness. I type back, *The job is a hard limit. What else?*

Anal?

No deal. I'm fucking that cute ass of yours, or we're not playing.

Eek.

I chuckle out loud. My room suddenly feels like a bedroom again, not this empty space where I lay my body at night.

Hurting me? Another text immediately follows. *And no sex with other people.*

No one else, I text back. *For either of us.* I send it then send another missive. *I will only hurt you in ways you like.*

The phone is silent for a moment, then she texts, *When do we start?*

Now I finally indulge in fisting my greedy cock. Giving it a hard tug, I close my eyes and let a thousand dirty scenarios involving Chelle run through my mind.

Then I remember I have the poker game tomorrow.

Damn.

But it's okay, I have all month with her.

I'll have a key to my place delivered to your office. I want you naked in my bed when I get home from my game tomorrow night. Understood?

Oh my God, she texts back, and a laugh rockets out of my throat. I pump my fist over my cock and close my eyes, thinking about Chelle, naked, here. When I come, I'm still smiling.

9

Chelle

The next morning I'm practically giddy. It's not about my arrangement with Nikolai—definitely not that. It's that I scored the deal with the skateboarders, and they want me to be their publicist not Janette.

Okay, maybe it's both.

I should be terrified about the Nikolai thing.

I literally did make a deal with the devil.

But I can't find it in me to be afraid. Nikolai just isn't that scary to me. I mean, logically, he is. I know what he did to Zane was violent. But it's possible it wasn't merciless. He seems to operate by a code or set of rules, and I don't think they involve hurting me or selling me to sex traffickers.

I'm not entirely sure what those rules are though.

Even though I'm operating on four hours of sleep, I take an extra long time in the shower, shaving everywhere and thinking about all the things that might happen tonight.

I will definitely be getting laid. I climb out of the

shower and smear my mango-ginger butter lotion every-where, then put on my sexiest matching bra and panties—the black lacy ones. Of course, Nikolai probably won't even see them because I'm supposed to be naked when he gets home. And another *of course*—I have time after work to do this stuff. I don't have to do it now.

But I want to.

"Echo," I shout into the kitchen. "Play Flo Rida's 'Low'."

I guess I'm feeling sexy. It was my favorite high school party song. When it comes on, I'm lured to the kitchen still in just my bra and panties to hear it full-blast. I stand in front of the Echo like it's my dance partner and slide my hands down my body, singing at the top of my lungs, slapping my booty and dropping into a squat at the appropriate times.

When "Low" is over, I ask Echo to play Katy Perry's "Teenage Dream," and I bebop to my bedroom to get dressed while singing like I'm thirteen.

I call Shanna on the way to work, even though I know she's still asleep. I can't help it. I have to leave a message on her voice mail. Somehow, I think she'd be proud of me.

"Well, I'm taking your advice. I'm finally having some gratuitous sex. Which is kind of a stupid term. Like when is sex not necessary? Oh, I guess gratuitous also means free. Well, this sex isn't free. It's worth thirty thousand dollas." Yes, I'm talking like a gangster. Or a thirteen-year-old. I'm being ridiculous, but it feels great.

I haven't had this much fun in a long time.

I guess Shanna really was right.

"Call me for the deets when you wake up," I sing into the phone then end the call with a goofy smile on my face.

Yep, that's right, bitches. Today is my day. I'll be bargaining for a promotion at work, and I brokered a deal worth thirty grand to get my brother off the hook. A deal that includes me getting laid on the regular for thirty nights.

Do I sound like a dude right now? I sort of feel like a dude.

Who knew all I needed was a little no-strings-attached sex to feel this empowered?

~

Nikolai

I'm in love.

I rewind the video feed of Chelle dancing around the kitchen in her bra and panties five times with my dick in my hand.

She's so. Damn. Hot.

And adorable.

And goofy. It's the goofiness that really disarms me. I liked uptight firecracker Chelle a lot. But seeing her with her guard down? It gets under my skin.

Makes me desperate for her to reveal that side of herself to me. To let her hair down. To be vulnerable. To look so happy and carefree.

Was it landing the deal with Skate 32 that made her so chipper this morning? Or was it our deal?

I hadn't found it in myself to regret the deal yet, and now I'm even more satisfied with my decision, even though I already know it won't end well.

At least there will be plenty of orgasms along the way, right?

Chelle texts me at lunch time. I'm upstairs, sitting at the breakfast bar with Sasha and Maxim. *What about my spin classes?*

I smile. *I am open to negotiation. You can earn privileges.*

She writes back, *Does that include going to the Red Room Wednesdays to see my BFF?*

The memory of her getting hit on by that *mudak* makes me grind my teeth. *No fucking chance. Not without me, anyway.*

Are you buying?

Now she's flirting. My smile returns. *If I take you out, I'm buying. But you haven't earned it yet.*

Sasha snatches my phone from my hand.

"Hey!"

"You're texting a woman!" she declares. "Is she the one from Rue's last night?"

I hold my hand out. "Give me the phone, Sasha. It's none of your fucking business."

"Watch your mouth with my wife," Maxim growls at me.

I ignore him because we both know she's being a pain. *Brat* is Sasha's middle name, but she's hot as fuck and came with oil wells worth sixty million dollars, so Maxim doesn't mind their arranged marriage thing.

She tries unsuccessfully to unlock my phone. "I saw, *If I take you out, I'm buying,*" she announces triumphantly. "So what's the deal? Are you dating this woman? Hmm?"

"Yes, what is the deal?" Story appears from Oleg's bedroom with my giant bratva brother behind her. "Last night was a strange scene. How did that even happen?"

I shake my head. I'm not as tempted to tell Story to mind her own fucking business because she's too kind and also because Oleg would legit kill me.

Oleg outs me, though, signing, *She is the sister of a guy who owes us money.* Story interprets out loud because she knows sign language best although the rest of us get the jist of it now without her interpretation.

Sasha, who majored in theatre, gives an exaggerated

gasp and claps a hand over her mouth. "Nikolai! *Gospodi,* did you take his sister as payment?"

Maxim grunts, and I realize they're all staring at me waiting for my answer. Like they think it's true.

The fact that it is pretty close to the truth burns me.

"Shut up. All of you. My arrangement with Chelle is none of your business."

"Oh. My. God." Sasha sounds delighted. "I can't believe it. You *did*!"

"I thought we had a no sex as currency rule," Maxim says mildly. Like he's not going to sweat me for it, but he's curious why I broke the rules. He's right, of course. The thirty grand Zane owes isn't mine to fuck with. It belongs to the bratva. I pay Adrian and Oleg out of it and a percentage always goes to Ravil.

"Stop." I make my voice as cutting as I can.

It only works because I'm the guy who never raises his voice. It's hard to get a rise out of me over much of anything.

But Chelle will be here, in this building, for the next thirty days. I can't keep any secrets from the bratva. Not without shit blowing up in my face.

"I made a deal," I admit. "But if one of you *mudaks* says one word to her about it, I will kill you. Understand?"

Sasha smiles but makes a show out of zipping her lips, locking them and throwing the key over her shoulder.

Story's brows are down, like she doesn't like it, and I suddenly feel like the worst kind of bastard.

I scrub a hand over my face. "Don't judge, please. I like this girl."

Story's face clears. All of them soften, in fact. Like I suddenly became the subject of their empathy, rather than the criminal who took someone's sister as payment for a debt to the mob.

"We'll be nice," Sasha promises. "I didn't talk to her much last night, but she seemed cool. Maybe I can hire her publicity firm for the theatre's next show."

A thread of relief flows through me. They're dropping the inquisition and accepting Chelle into the fold, just like that.

It's one of the many miracles of my life in Ravil's cell. They are family in the best sense of the word. I don't know why I was feeling like I didn't belong lately.

"Yeah, and what's the deal with Skate 32?" Story pipes in. "Do you think they'll really use our music in their videos?"

I shrug. "I don't know, but I'm sure Chelle would try to make it happen if you're into it."

I think that's true. I hope so, anyway.

I catch Oleg's eye. "You ready to do some enforcing?" I ask. It's Friday, which means we make the rounds to collect money we're owed.

I don't think Oleg loves his job, but he's stoic as ever. He nods, then signs to Story and gives her a kiss.

For the first time since Dima left, I don't feel the sharp stab of jealousy at witnessing that intimacy. The sense of being left out.

Because tonight, I won't be sleeping alone.

10

Chelle

As promised, a very tattooed courier with a thick Russian accent showed up at my work to deliver an envelope for me this afternoon. Inside was a keycard and a note written in Nikolai's neat, square letters.

Chelle,

I look forward to having you as my sex slave.

I'm in Suite 1110. You'll need the keycard for the elevator and my door. You can also use it to park in the garage beneath the building.

I want you there by nine, but don't expect me home until after midnight.

—N

I READ and reread that first line twenty times. How seriously is he taking this sex slave thing?

Well, obviously, seriously, considering the texts we exchanged. I think it's the word "slave" that's throwing me.

But knowing Nikolai—*do I know Nikolai?*—he's being

tongue-in-cheek. The guy doesn't strike me as hard-core anything.

Then again, I saw my brother's face after he visited him.

Oh, and he did go back to break his nose after Zane took the ring from my purse and almost got me fired. I couldn't find it in me to resent that one, much. He had it coming.

At four o'clock, the skateboarders come out of the conference room and over to my desk.

"Cheeeeeeeeelle! Come here and give me some sugar." Randy holds his arms out for a hug.

I stand and let him pick me up off the ground in a bear hug. "Good thing Nikolai isn't here, or he'd break my legs, right?" he jokes, probably not realizing how true it might be.

Still, I don't mind it today. What felt slightly threatening and icky yesterday all seems in good fun now. We're friends. They want me as their publicist. They think I'm cool.

"We said we wanted you, or we wouldn't sign," Randy says in a low voice as he puts me back down on my feet.

"And?" I ask, breathless.

"And it's done." He beams. "Get us in touch with Flynn's band, okay?"

"I will," I promise as Bones gives me the same pick-up and spin me around treatment.

"Hey, just because I'm small doesn't mean you can manhandle me," I point out.

"I won't manhandle you," Tiny promises, holding out his hand, but when I go to shake it, he rushes in for the bear hug.

"Bye, thanks for a good time," he says when he drops me back on my feet.

I shake my head. "You guys are going to be a pain in my ass, aren't you?"

All three grin at me. "You know it!" They point and make pseudo-gang gestures as they back away from my desk. I roll my eyes.

When they leave, I grow a pair and knock on Janette's door.

"Well, I guess you impressed them," she says.

"I haven't told you how much I spent for dinner," I say, wincing. "They insisted on the best sushi restaurant in town and then ordered drink after drink and plate after plate."

"What was the damage? You know what?" She holds up a manicured hand. Her plum-colored nails look elegant against her dark skin. "I don't even want to know. I got them signed on for a two-year contract, so it's all good. But next time they want sushi they can treat you. They certainly make enough money."

I latch onto her words, *they can treat you.*

"So…" I cock my head, trying to figure out how to phrase my question.

"So, it looks like you're my new Junior Publicist. Congratulations."

I beam at her. "Thank you. I'm thrilled. These guys are a handful, but I have ideas for them. I think I can really help define their brand and get it out there."

"Oh, I have no doubt about the creative part. It's the fact that you managed them that impressed me. The customer-client relationship is just as important as the work we do for our clients, and that's the piece I wasn't sure you were ready for. But I was wrong." She lifts her brows and smiles. "I'll put a contract together for you over the weekend. Your first task Monday morning needs to be hiring me a new assistant. You're going to be hard to replace in that department."

I stand. "Thank you. Are you okay if I leave early? I had a late night with the skate-boys, and I'm wiped."

She tips her head. "Well, you look great, but sure. See you Monday."

I grab my purse from my desk and head out.

Time to head to my second job. The one where I answer to a bossy Russian. I climb in the elevator and ignore the way my nipples tighten and burn thinking about him.

About his orders for tonight.

About taking my clothes off for him.

Waiting in bed for Nikolai to come home and find me waiting.

Naked.

Ready.

Wet.

Nikolai

Longest. Fucking. Poker night. Ever.

I was ready to be done before it even started, and now that it's finally wrapping up, I can barely contain my irritation. To make it worse, Dima didn't come to Chicago this weekend, so being here feels especially meaningless.

"What's your rush?" Adrian asks when I snap at him to pick it up.

Oleg signs to him that I have a woman waiting—or something like that.

"I liked it better when you didn't talk," I grump at him, then instantly regret it, because I know it takes effort for our mute brother to even attempt to participate in conversation. "I'm just kidding, man." I punch him lightly on the shoulder. "Sort of."

He shakes his head at me, then signs, *you go*.

"Can I go?" I look around. He and Adrian almost have everything wrapped up.

"Why not?" Adrian asks. He's young, but he fits into our cell. He's fearless and brutal. He's not afraid to get his hands dirty. And he's smart. He got caught torching the factory where his sister was held prisoner, but he's learned since then how to avoid criminal charges. Under Maxim's direction, he's become the bratva cleaner. The guy who goes in to erase all evidence from a crime scene.

"I'm going to leave then. Thanks, guys. I'll pay you out tomorrow when I finish the accounting." That's another drawback of not having Dima here.

I take the elevator to the underground parking lot. It's one in the morning. Chelle will definitely be asleep. My cock stirs as I try to guess whether she followed my directions or not. She's a little spark plug, so I wouldn't be surprised if she gives me pushback everywhere she can. Then again, she probably won't want to test me first thing.

I park beneath the building and take the elevator. It suddenly makes sense why I moved to this floor. Not that I knew something like this would happen, but I made the space for it, didn't I?

Keeping Chelle in my bedroom and trotting her out in front of everyone all month would've been a pain in my ass. The other guys have managed it, but it's not my style.

Besides, the other guys didn't plan on letting their women go when they brought them into the penthouse. My deal with Chelle has an expiration date. Which means I can't show her anything about the organization, or she'll become a liability.

Ravil may have my nuts over this as it is. I didn't exactly ask for permission.

I key into my place. The lights are all off, but the feel is completely different.

It's not vacuous.

I'm not alone.

My cock stirs as I walk to the bedroom. I enter and turn on the light in the en suite bathroom to provide a gentle glow to the room. Chelle is on her side facing the wall, curled into a little ball. I stand at the dresser and remove my jacket, shoes, and watch.

Chelle doesn't move, but I suspect she's not asleep. I walk over to her side of the bed and pull the covers down just enough to see if she's naked. She is. Beautifully so. She's just wearing a delicate gold chain around her neck with a diamond-studded Star of David attached. She doesn't move.

Definitely awake.

I lean down and kiss her bare shoulder. "Hey, beautiful."

She opens her eyes, but looks straight ahead instead of up at me. Something tightens in my chest.

I'm an asshole for making this deal.

I stroke my hand down her side. Her skin is so soft and smooth. "Don't be scared, little bunny. I won't hurt you."

Now she looks up at me. "I'm not scared. It—it's just been a minute. You know, since I've had—"

"You don't have to perform," I interrupt, absurdly pleased that she hasn't had sex with anyone in a long time. "You just have to obey. I'll tell you what I want."

She rolls onto her back, and I twitch the sheet down, so I can see her breasts in all their glory.

She catches it but doesn't tug it back up, her gaze tangling with mine and holding. Her breath stops.

I brush my thumb across the peak of one nipple, and it pebbles. Her legs swish under the covers. "Put your hand between your legs, *zayka*. Show me how you touch yourself." I pull the covers down to her thighs and then pace away to give her some space. Standing at the foot of the bed, I slowly unbutton my shirt while Chelle bends one knee up and slides her middle finger between her legs.

I take off my button-down then tug the undershirt over my head. Chelle pushes up on one elbow to watch me. Her gaze dances over my torso then lands on my fresh scar. The last thing I want her to focus on for a variety of reasons.

"Is that... a gunshot wound?"

"Yes."

"It looks new."

"It is. No more questions." I unbuckle my belt and slide it from the loops, then slide off my slacks and boxers.

Her attention goes to my very sizable erection rather than the scar.

All for you, little bunny.

"Protection," Chelle says quickly in a rusty voice. "That should've been a hard limit."

"I'll protect you," I promise. "Are you wet?"

She licks her lips, her fingers working between her legs. "Um... a little. Not all the way there yet."

I step forward and lower my forearms to the bed, pushing both her knees up and open. I take one long swipe of my tongue up her slit then lift my head to watch her reaction.

Seeing nothing but lust in her expression, I slide my hands under her ass to lift her to my mouth, so I can feast on her sweet, feminine folds. I suck her labia, lick all around them, nip her outer lips, her inner thighs. I squeeze and knead her ass and work my thumb into her pussy while I suck her clit.

"Nikolai," she gasps. "Oh!"

"Hmm," I murmur with satisfaction. "Now you're wet."

"Yes." Her hips buck beneath my lips.

"Don't come, Freckles. Not until I give you permission, understand?"

She nods, brows down. "Okay."

This isn't a game I've played before, but I'm not oblivious to the master-slave fetish. I didn't know I was into it until now, but then again, I've never had my own personal sex slave before.

I'm suddenly not sure why I've denied myself for so long.

Later, another night, I will lick her sweet pussy until she comes, but tonight I can't wait any longer. I've had blue balls all day, even though I jacked off watching her dance around in her bra and panties this morning.

I sit back and withdraw my thumb. Chelle blinks those golden eyes at me. I like having her gaze pinned to me this way—so attentive. So present.

"Roll over, pretty girl, and spread your legs." I get up to grab a condom from the nightstand.

She scrambles to comply, turning over to lie flat on her belly and spreading her legs wide.

"Good girl."

I rip open the condom package and roll the rubber on as I climb over her. I run my palm over her ass. There aren't any marks from the spanking I gave her Wednesday. I can't decide if I'm relieved or disappointed.

I liked seeing my handprints on her as much as I loved the way she squirmed and made those sweet little sex sounds while I spanked her.

I give her ass a light slap now, and she rolls her hips. I kneel between her legs and rub the head of my dick over her entrance. She's juicy, her flesh plump and slick. Welcoming.

She is tight, though, so I go slowly. She moans softly as I fill her.

"You feel that, Freckles?" I say, my brain scrambling with the pleasure of arcing in and out of her. It's not just the physical sensation although that's incredible. It's the entire situation. It's the fact that it's Chelle and that we've made this deal. I push in deeper, picking up to a careful, even rhythm. "That's the cock you're going to come all over," I tell her. "But not until I give you permission. Understand?"

She doesn't answer.

"Do I need to make you call me *master*, little bunny?"

"No," she gasps. "Sorry. I understand."

"Good girl." My cock swells even more with pleasure. I won't last long.

I shove in harder, but she's so light I scoot her up the bed with each thrust. I grip her nape to hold her in place. She gets even wetter, like that turns her on.

"You like being held down, Chelle?" I ask.

Her pussy's molten now, deliciously slick but tight.

"Hmm?"

"Maybe. I think so," she gasps. She arches her ass up to meet my thrusts, making her slender back curve in the most delicious way.

I chuckle. "I think so, too. I'll definitely be tying you to this bed, little bunny."

Her pussy clenches around my cock.

"Uh oh. You're not trying to come are you?"

"I—I, oh God." She orgasms.

"Bad girl." I fuck her harder. Faster.

Her fingers twist into the sheets. She lifts her head. "*Yes... yes.*" She sounds desperate even though she's already come. Maybe I didn't let her finish.

Too bad. She broke my rules. It's all about my climax now. I put a snap into my hips, slapping her ass with my loins, driving deep with a brutal force.

"*Blyad.' Blyad'!*" I shout as my balls draw up tight. I slam in deep and fill the condom with the most satisfying orgasm I've had in years. Maybe ever.

Chelle comes too, her internal muscles squeezing and pulsing around my dick, making me come even harder.

I don't want to ever stop, it feels so good. I close my eyes and savor it, then withdraw and shove into her again to wring a little more pleasure out of both of us.

"Next time you disobey me, I'm going to fuck that cute little ass of yours," I growl, lowering my head down to bite her shoulder.

She climaxes a little more, and I'm flooded with warmth and affection for her. I kiss down the column of her neck as I settle between her legs for a moment. She makes a soft humming sound that seems to fill all the empty spaces in my heart.

I don't know why I care so much about her satisfaction when I made the deal for me. But then, that might be a lie. I may have made the deal all for her. Because she wanted to have sex with me without it counting. And she wanted her brother out from under my thumb.

I'm the one who had rules against accepting sex in trade. I'm the one who wanted more than sex.

I'm going to have to watch out. Chelle Goldberg may be at my beck and call, but I'm the one who's wrapped firmly around her little finger.

11

Chelle

I sleep until ten. I'm not used to sleeping naked. Or waking up sore and well-used. It all feels deliciously dirty.

I stretch in Nikolai's wonderfully comfortable bed and look around. He's not in the bedroom. I hear rustling coming from the living room.

Part of me wants to hide here in the bedroom. Maybe go back to sleep and delay the awkwardness, but I find myself magnetized to Nikolai's presence. Even though I packed two suitcases of my own clothes, I open his drawers until I find one of his soft undershirts, and I pull it on and pad to the living room.

If I'd forgotten overnight what Nikolai is, it all comes rushing back. He's devastatingly sexy, looking freshly showered and dressed. He's sitting on his couch with a laptop and stacks of cash in front of him. I shove down the judgement and anxiety his occupation brings and walk over. "On a scale of one to ten, how illegal is what you do?" I ask, waving a hand at the money.

His sexy lips quirk. "Come here." He holds an arm out to me.

I walk over, and he tugs me onto his lap, his hands immediately exploring under the t-shirt. I squirm as he cups one breast at the same time he strokes my upper thigh.

"You look beautiful in my shirt," he murmurs, his teeth scoring my shoulder.

I squirm some more, getting turned on by his obvious attraction for me.

"I was going to insist you stay naked when you're in my apartment, but I guess I'll let you leave it on for now."

I squeeze my thighs together, both turned on and offended by his words. All I can manage to say is, "Meep."

I never considered he would make me stay naked. I really didn't know what to expect when we made this arrangement. My imagination couldn't conjure much more than being tied up or spanked again.

Both of those scenarios excite me.

The idea of being forced to be naked shocks me, but it also makes me wet and hot, so I guess on some level I must like it.

"What do you like for breakfast? I have yogurt. Or eggs. Or we can order in."

"I usually eat yogurt," I tell him, sliding off his lap. I decide to act like I own the place rather than slink around and ask permission. I open his refrigerator and find my favorite brand and flavor of yogurt— the Greek kind with mango chunks. "This yogurt's great," I tell him as I crack it open.

I find a spoon and walk back to the living room to watch him place wraps on the money and stack it up.

"How much did you make?" I drop onto the sofa beside him.

"Twenty. Not a great night." He shrugs. "And I shouldn't have told you that. Don't ask me about business again, okay? It's for your own protection. You don't want to become a potential witness or an accessory."

My heart thuds against my breastbone, that fight-or-flight cold washing over me. I can't decide if I'm scared for myself or for him.

He looks at me. "It's low on the scale." I realize he's answering my earlier question. "Hardly illegal at all."

I eat my yogurt slowly, savoring the smooth creaminess. "How did you get into the mafia?"

"Bratva."

"What?"

"Russian *mafiya* is called bratva. For brotherhood. My brother and I were recruited out of secondary."

"What is secondary? Like middle school?"

Nikolai's forehead wrinkles. "No, it's the end of schooling. You call it high school, I guess."

"How old were you?"

"Seventeen." The money is stacked, and Nikolai shuts the laptop and sits back. "My brother's girlfriend was dying of cancer. He heard about this treatment. You know, he thought it could save her life. I got the bratva to loan us the money." He shrugs. "Of course, we couldn't pay it back. The trade was for our lives."

My breakfast sinks to the bottom of my stomach. I don't know why I never considered how Nikolai got in. I sort of made the assumption that he likes money and flashy cars and sex with lots of women, and that's why he does what he does.

I digest everything he said. "So you and your brother are twins?" I remember the guy who looked just like him, except with glasses, from the hotel suite.

"*Da.*"

"What's his name?"

"Dima."

"And what happened with his girlfriend?"

"Dead."

I figured, but it still makes me sad. "I'm sorry."

"It was a long time ago. He has a new girlfriend now. They moved away a few months ago, so she could go to school."

Once more, Nikolai becomes sharply in focus as a three-dimensional human. I realize he sounded a little wooden on the last part and reach out to touch his knee. "Is that hard for you?"

He doesn't answer for a moment, which is answer enough. I would imagine in his line of business they don't like to show weakness. Not that missing your twin brother is a weakness. "It's all right," he says slowly. "They come back most weekends, and I see him on video calls. But yeah, it's not the same." He looks toward the stunning view of the lake. "It's not so much that I miss him, as I…" He trails off and shakes his head, like he wants to dismiss the whole conversation.

I catch his hand in mine. The gesture feels both shocking and familiar. I mean, I had sex with this guy last night, but we're not exactly intimate. We're not lovers; we're just sex partners. I think I'm more surprised at my instinct to hold his hand than anything. "What?" I ask softly, even though I know if he answers, if he tells me his innermost rumblings, we'll diverge into something else.

Beyond sex.

He looks at me, that suggestive naughtiness in the hint of his smile. "I need a hobby now."

My nipples tighten. "So I'm that hobby for the month?" I guess.

His smile stretches, making him look more boyish.

"Exactly, Freckles. Torturing you will be my entertainment."

Bubbles of excitement fizz and pop inside me.

"Speaking of which, have you told Zane he doesn't owe me any payments for now? Otherwise, he's going to be robbing some other girl of expensive rings."

I hesitate. "Do you want me to let him know?"

"No," I say quickly. Zane will probably flip out over this. "I'll do it." I take my yogurt container and spoon to the kitchen then go to the bedroom to text Zane.

I made a deal with Nikolai. You don't have to worry about making payments anymore.

I know Nikolai said, for now, but that's because he's not cancelling the debt until I've completed the full thirty days. After last night, I'm certain I won't fail. Sex with Nikolai is no hardship. Neither is living in his gorgeous apartment.

Yes, I'm at his beck and call, and he will probably make me do all kinds of things I've never tried, but that gets me hot. I'm the kind of person who needs to have boundaries pushed or I'd never try anything.

No, the hardest thing about spending a month under Nikolai's rule will be not getting emotionally involved.

Zane calls immediately.

Dammit.

I don't really want to pick up. I don't want to go into this with him. But if I don't, he'll keep calling. I answer the call.

"Hi."

"What did you do?" Fear rings in his voice.

"Don't worry about it. I'm taking care of things. You just keep your nose out of the coke and get your grades back on track."

"*Chelle.* What did you do?"

"I made a deal with Nikolai. Everything is fine."

"*What. Deal?*"

"You don't need to know the details. It's nothing horrible."

"The hell it's not! You don't know these guys! Chelle, is it sex? Did you whore—"

I end the call, hot tears spearing my eyes. Now I feel like a whore. What felt fun and exciting a minute ago now feels shameful, dark, and dirty.

"He flipped out, didn't he?" Nikolai stands in the bedroom doorway, watching me.

I blink rapidly, trying to shove the tears back down my throat. "Yeah, well. He's afraid of you."

"No, he's pissed. I would probably think less of him if he wasn't. I'll let him punch my face when I see him. I deserve it."

Nikolai's words don't make me feel better. Not at all. I stare at him bleakly.

"Hey." He crosses the room and reaches for me. When I hug myself with my arms, he settles his hands on my waist and tries to catch my gaze. "You're safe with me. You know that, right?"

I try to swallow down the lump in my throat.

"You're not a prisoner. You can leave any time."

Gah. The tears won't stop threatening to spill. My jaw works, trying to keep it all in.

"See, this is why sex shouldn't be a transaction," he says with an exasperated exhale. "Are you feeling cheap?"

One tear spills down my cheek, and I finally drag my gaze up to his face. He brushes it away with his thumb. "You're the one who wouldn't invite me up," he accuses.

I can't help it—a watery laugh tumbles out of my lips.

For just a minute, I let myself imagine what would've happened if I'd invited him up. But I can't. Because I wouldn't. Nikolai is not a guy I would actually date, and I don't do casual sex.

Our gazes lock and hold, and the corners of Nikolai's lips curve. "Come on. You like the idea of being my slave. There's nothing to be ashamed of."

The tight fist clenching beneath my ribs loosens. Some of the sexiness I felt as a result of our deal flows back in. Gratitude for his ability to throw that switch in me washes the rest of the shame and judgement away. I reach for his face and pull it down to mine, giving him a kiss. I suddenly want to climb him like a tree. To reward him for being so damn *kind* to me through this whole process. From the minute I barged in on his game trying to give him my car until now, he's been a hundred times more considerate than I've expected.

His hand cups my ass as he returns the kiss. "What was that for?" he asks when we break apart.

"I just… it was a thank you. Because you've been amazing."

"Amazing, huh?" He unbuttons his jeans. "Why don't you show me your gratitude?"

I lick my lips, the nerves I had last night returning as I sink to my knees in front of him. It's not that I don't know how to give a blowjob. I totally do. I think I'm pretty good at it. I just want Nikolai to think so.

You don't have to perform. His words from last night echo against the walls I built for myself, and I'm filled with even more gratitude. I grasp the base of his cock and stroke it.

His cock lengthens in my grasp, bobbing for me. I flick my tongue against his frenulum and then swirl it there.

"That's it, little bunny. Let me see that pretty mouth of yours stretch around my cock."

I lift my gaze to his and hold it as I part my lips and slowly take him into my mouth. He shudders, his balls drawing up and releasing, his cock thickening and length-ening even more. I taste the salt of his essence as I concentrate my sucking around the head then take him deeper, into the pocket of my cheek.

"Mmm, that's so hot, Freckles. You look so good when you suck my dick."

His words are crass, but they turn me on. I attempt to take him deeper, into the back of my throat. I'm not good at it—I usually gag, but I want to try. He holds still, and I go slowly, working on relaxing the muscles of my throat to take him deeper, deeper.

When I lift my gaze again, he's right there with me, watching closely like he understands I was testing my own boundaries. I pop off for a minute to let my jaw relax.

"*Now* I'm going to need that shirt to come off." He tugs it over my head, then pinches one of my nipples. "You have the sweetest tits."

I cover them with my hands. "By sweetest, do you mean smallest?"

He pulls my fingers away and holds them taut above my head, pinned together with one hand. With the other, he slaps the side of one of my breasts lightly two times—a punitive little spank. "I mean perfect." He pinches the other nipple and holds it clamped between his fingers, which makes me gasp as my pussy grows slick.

When he releases my hands, I return to my job, grasping his cock and feeding his length into my mouth. I swirl my tongue underneath it, then use my hand to pump as I take him in and out, so it feels like all of him is in. All the while, my hips undulate and swirl, my own arousal growing stronger with every bit of pleasure I give.

"You're so pretty on your knees." Nikolai gathers my hair at the back of my head, then uses it to push my face over his cock. He's in control now—nothing for me to do, but follow his lead. It's degrading, but I love it. I like feeling used by him, an object for his pleasure.

I don't want to unpack why or what it says about me.

Nikolai's movements grow faster, jerkier. More frantic. I hold onto his powerful thighs for stability, and I feel them shake as he grows close to climax. "Are you going to be a good girl and swallow?"

I attempt to nod around the cock stuffed in my mouth, humming my agreement, even though I've never managed to swallow before.

Nikolai says something in Russian that sounds like a curse, then lets out a string of words before his balls draw up tight, and he comes. His cum is hot and salty hitting the back of my throat. I pull off in surprise, reminding myself to relax my gag reflex. I swallow it down, then take him into my mouth to suck again, drawing another orgasm from him.

He continues to speak in Russian, caressing my head and stroking my cheek. Then he grasps my elbows and pulls me to stand. "Come here, little bunny. I know you need to come, too." He bends me over the edge of the bed and gives my ass a flurry of slaps.

All I can do is let out cries of surprise—ohs and ahs—as the shock mingles pleasure with pain.

"Stay there, *zayka*. Don't move."

I obey, my face buried in the soft covers of his bed. I hear him open a drawer, but I don't look. There's something about the anticipation—not knowing what he's going to do with me—that makes this moment all the hotter.

He can't screw me because he just orgasmed, so what will it be? What is he planning?

He returns and slaps my ass a few more times, making me jump and buck. When he runs his fingers between my legs, I hear the slickness of my arousal coating my flesh.

He pries my cheeks apart and I jolt with surprise. "Hold still, bunny," he instructs. A drop of something cold lands between my cheeks, and he massages it over my anus.

My heart beats hard against my ribs. I both want this and don't want it at the same time. It's scary and exciting. A cool metal object pressed against my anus.

I tighten and try to straighten, but Nikolai pushes my torso back down.

"Relax, Freckles. I'm going to plug your ass, and you're going to like it. I have to get you ready for my cock."

I'm still not so sure, but he's applying gentle pressure at my back entrance.

"Exhale and push," he instructs.

I hold my breath for a moment as I struggle to accept what's happening. But even as I resist, the pleasure of having my anus probed takes over the shame of it. I force myself to relax and push, as he ordered, and the plug slides forward.

"Oh! Ohhh," I moan as it stretches me.

"Take it, Chelle." He dribbles more lube over the plug and teases me with it, fucking my ass with the end.

It feels wonderful. Horrible and wonderful. I love-hate it.

My pussy feels far too empty, and I reach my arm underneath me to touch it.

"That's right, *zayka*. Play with that pretty pussy while I play with your ass. You have permission to come whenever you're ready."

Permission to come.

I'd already forgotten his rule from last night. The one I broke.

My fingers sink into my pussy without me even trying —I'm so wet and plump down there it's like a foreign land.

Nikolai fucks me with the plug, teasing my ass for a series of pumps before pushing it a little deeper each time. Stretching me wider with each go.

I moan, feverish with the need to come but not ready yet. I have to hold too still for Nikolai; I want more in my pussy. But it all feels so good. So deliriously satisfying in the most hedonistic way possible. Nikolai pushes the bulbous plug in all the way, which is both a relief and a disappointment, because I want more. But he's not done. He continues to fuck me with it, pulling it out and pushing it in. I plunge my own fingers inside my pussy—multiple fingers. I've never felt myself this way—like a freaking river down there!

"Please," I start to beg. "Please, Nikolai. Oh, please."

He growls and kicks my legs wider. "Move your fingers." His roughened voice gets me even hotter. I move my fingers, and he starts to slap my pussy—short, sharp slaps over my folds, hitting my clit. They sting and satisfy in a way my own fingers hadn't. When he coordinates it with the ass-fucking, I completely lose my mind.

I start begging, or maybe screaming. Definitely making noises I can't control.

Nikolai spanks harder, and I yip, then frantically reach for my pussy with both hands, bucking over my fingers as I come harder than I've ever come in my life.

When it's over, I nearly pass out. I'm dizzy and limp and completely wrung out.

Nikolai lifts me the rest of the way to the bed, and I lie there with my mind blown for what could have been hours. Maybe it was only minutes.

I really don't know.

All I know is that my world just expanded in ways I didn't think were possible.

I finally manage to roll myself onto my back and blink my eyes open.

"There you are." Nikolai holds out a glass of water. It takes effort just to push myself onto my forearms to drink.

"That was insane," I pant between sips.

Nikolai's smile is smug.

"I'm just getting started, Freckles."

12

Nikolai

I'M FINDING it hard to regret my bad decision-making. Watching Chelle come undone was a fucking privilege.

I take care of business while Chelle showers—paying Oleg, Adrian and Ravil out of the pot, then I order some gyros and Greek salad to be delivered for lunch.

"You need a dining table," Chelle announces when the food arrives, and I put it on the quartz breakfast bar.

"Do I?" I survey the apartment. I guess a dining table seemed pointless when it's just me living here. "I rearranged many times but nothing seemed right," I admit, waving my arm around the open-concept living area. "Where would I put it?"

"By the windows. Definitely." There's a warm timbre to her voice that does something strange to my insides.

"You'll have to pick it out for me," I tell her. "That's your next assignment."

"I get assignments, huh? That's how this works?" I love the flirty lilt of her words.

"You do what you're told. That's all." My words are harsh, but my tone is easy, as always.

"I thought it was just sex." She looks at me from under her lashes. She's wearing mascara and light makeup, which for some reason turns me on. Maybe because she made an effort for me.

"It's whatever the hell I want. Come and eat." I pull back one of the barstools at the breakfast counter. The design of my suite is similar to the penthouse upstairs, only half the size.

She hops onto the stool and opens the bag of food. "You don't cook much, do you?" She pops open a styrofoam container and makes an approving sound.

"I heat things in the microwave," I tell her. "I can cook eggs. That's about it. Do you like to cook?" I suddenly wish I'd had more time to stalk her on her Echo. Like I've missed out on all the things that make Chelle's life, and I want to catch up.

"I like to cook," she says. "Brunch is my favorite."

"Brunch. What do you make for brunch?"

She smiles. "You know—breakfast food. Frittatas or quiche. Or ricotta pancakes. Fruit salad. Mimosas."

An unfamiliar feeling stirs in my gut. Something like jealousy, which makes no sense.

"Who do you make this brunch for?" I sound far grumpier than usual.

She shrugs. "Zane. Or Shanna, my friend from the Red Room." She picks up the gyro and squeezes it together to take a bite.

The jealousy remains. "Tomorrow you'll make me brunch." My imperious tone makes me sound like a total dick, but I can't help myself. I want to be the recipient of her attention. Her food.

Fortunately, she doesn't catch the asshole in my voice. Either that, or she really does like to cook brunch, because she perks up. "Okay. I need to go shopping because you don't have much in the fridge."

I nod. "We'll go shopping together."

"Are we shopping for furniture, too? Or do I do that on my own?"

Another unpleasant streak of anger runs through me. "We'll go together."

Blyad.'

I identify the feeling. Possessiveness. I'd felt it at the Red Room that night when the guy talked to her at the bar. Now I'm pissy about her giving her time or attention to anyone but me.

What in the hell is wrong with me?

I've never been possessive of a woman in my life. In fact, I usually can't wait to bail as soon as we've had sex.

No wonder I've broken all my rules when it comes to her. There's something different about her, for sure. She's captivated me. This surliness I feel is the same way Dima got with Natasha. Especially because he didn't think he could have her.

Fuck.

The realization that I'm in the same fucking boat hits me like a sucker punch to the gut.

"What?" Chelle asks.

I immediately make my expression blank. It is what it is. A transaction. Thirty days for her brother's note. Chelle doesn't want a relationship with me, she's already made that clear.

The dark jealousy rumbles in the pit of my stomach again.

"I'm just planning all the ways I'm going to torture you, little bunny," I say darkly.

She stops chewing and squeezes her thighs together like she's turned on.

And that makes it all worth it. At least we both will have our sexual fantasies fulfilled. Making Chelle scream, even for a short time, is almost as satisfying as getting to keep her.

~

CHELLE

"So...what do I have to do to earn a spin class?" I crawl over Nikolai's lap to straddle him where he was sitting on the couch. I don't know when I became a seductress, but it's so far out of the box for me that it feels powerful and fun.

We visited a couple furniture stores without me finding anything suitable and stopped to pick up groceries for the week. I let Nikolai pay for them, of course.

Now Nikolai and I are on the sofa looking online for a dining room set.

He grabs my ass and grinds me over his erection. Based on the way his eyelids droop, I'm sure he's thinking of dozens of dirty things to order me to do, but then asks, "What's the point of spin? Riding a bike indoors? I don't get it."

"Well, there's an instructor and music and the whole energy of the class to keep you going. It's fun."

"Hmm."

Not the answer I was going for. I'm pretty much addicted to my spin class. I rely on the exercise and endorphins to get me through my week and keep me in shape. I seriously won't survive a month without spin class.

Okay, that's being overly dramatic, but it would suck. I'd rather come to an arrangement with Nikolai.

He loops a finger through the chain around my neck and fingers my little Star of David pendant.

"My dad gave it to me," I say as an explanation because I sense the question in his gesture. "It was a bat mitzvah gift."

Nikolai studies my face without comment. "Are you religious?"

I shrug. "No, but he's dead."

Nikolai nods. "I know."

"You know? How?"

"Your brother's been at my table for over a year now. It's my business to know the background of my clients."

I want to snort at the word client, but I sense sympathy in Nikolai's gaze, and it pokes my tender spot. "Do you know how he died?" The bitter taste of grief and remaining anger coat my mouth.

Nikolai nods again and strokes a thumb lightly across my cheek. "I'm sorry, *zayka*. It must've been hard for you when your brother is still so young."

Ack. He named it. Tears instantly pop into my eyes. "Yeah," I choke. "Especially…" I break off because, well, Nikolai is the cause of my current stress over Zane. Of course, it's Zane's fault, but Nikolai's the problem.

"Especially now?" he asks, guessing too much. "Zane's gambling habit must be hard to watch after what happened with your dad."

A sob rockets out of my throat, and I lurch to climb off his lap.

Nikolai catches my waist and pulls me back. "Don't run, Freckles," he murmurs. "I can take the tears. Let me have them."

It's a strange thing to say. I don't know if it's something

that doesn't translate the same from Russian, but it frees me. I punch his chest as I dissolve into a hysterical mess. He catches my wrists and tries to wrap his arms around me as I continue to struggle.

I haven't even admitted this terror out loud. That Zane will end up like my dad, putting a bullet into his own head because of his gambling problem. Now that Nikolai just spoke it aloud, it looms up, huge and ugly—the shadow monster I've been trying to keep under lock. The thing I've been trying so hard to keep at bay for both of us.

I punch his chest again. "It's your fault," I accuse, even though it's not true.

"I won't let him back, okay? Even after the debt is paid."

I throw myself against him, burying my wet face against his neck and wrapping my arms around his strong shoulders. "Thank you," I sob, knowing full well that Nikolai refusing to allow Zane back doesn't mean my brother won't find another form of gambling if he wants to.

Zane needs help.

More than I can provide.

Nikolai strokes his hands up and down my back. "I spent half my life trying to keep my brother alive when he wasn't sure he wanted to live," Nikolai says. "I know what it's like to be the one trying to keep the boat from flipping."

"I'm sorry." I move my lips against the soft skin of his neck. "I know this shit is Zane's fault, not yours."

"I play a part," Nikolai owns. "But you're innocent. It's not fair to make you pay."

I lift my head, wiping my tears with the back of my hand. "You're a good person, Nikolai. For a bad guy."

A sad ghost of a smile around his mouth appears. Like he agrees he's the bad guy but doesn't want to be.

He shrugs. "I tried to be good. But you were too tempting." His hands caress down my back and settle on my ass, where he gives a light squeeze.

I nuzzle into his neck and kiss him there. Light kisses that, like holding his hand, feel both shockingly intimate and easy at the same time. I kiss his jaw, his temple. I rock over his cock. I'm sore from last night and the butt plug this morning, but I could easily go again. This arrangement—or maybe it's just Nikolai, himself—has turned me into someone I hardly recognize. A wanton hedonist who has the power to both seduce and surrender.

"So about that spin class," I purr in his ear as I undulate over his lap.

"You'll have to earn it," he murmurs back, pulling my shirt over my head. "You're doing a great job, but you're not there yet."

I rock over his erection like he's already inside me. "No?" I make my voice velvet. "What would it take?"

He unsnaps my bra and pulls it off. "You're getting there. But you're still wearing clothes. Why is that?"

I slide backward off his lap and shimmy out of my jeans and panties while he unbuttons his pants and pulls a condom out of his back pocket. "Because I would've been arrested if we'd gone shopping naked," I say and spread my arms wide. "Problem solved."

"I want you naked in my apartment," he says as I straddle his waist. "Or close to it." He touches the star at my throat. "I would've made you wear my collar, but I don't want to fuck with that."

I pause as I digest that—the unexpected turn-on of hearing he wants to collar me like a pet as well as his consideration of my tribute to my father. I throw myself at him again, kissing his mouth, my tongue twining with his as he rolls a condom on and holds his cock steady for me to sink onto.

"That's it, *zayka*. Forget your spin class. You can ride me."

I laugh and bounce up and down over his cock, loving how powerful and sexy I feel. How interesting and admired.

No one has ever made me feel this way before.

I love it, and it destroys me at the same time.

Because I have to remember—this isn't real. It's thirty days to Zane's freedom.

Nikolai's a player, and this isn't real.

That doesn't mean I can't enjoy it while I'm here.

Nikolai holds my waist and helps me as I fatigue. I close my eyes, drop my head back to let my long hair brush my spine and just enjoy the delicious sensations.

After riding a peak, we slow our rhythm, and I change to a more circular undulation of my hips, grinding my clit against his loins. We breathe together. Time slows. Maybe it stops. We're suspended in this place of carnal pleasure. Nikolai pinches one of my nipples, rolling and tugging it between his fingers and then suddenly slow is not enough. I ride him in earnest, like my life depends on reaching that climax.

"Don't come until I give you permission," he reminds me.

"You're mean," I pant, getting close. So close.

"Be careful, or I won't let you come at all."

"Mean," I repeat. Maybe I'm half-goading him. I sort of loved that spanking he gave me the night I got drunk at the Red Room. It hurt, but it was hot.

I can tell he's getting close because he doesn't answer. His mouth is open, jaw slightly forward. "You're sexy when you're mean," I admit.

He pinches both my nipples at once, hard, and I cry out, my orgasm starting.

Nikolai grabs my hips and shoves up inside me at the same time he yanks me down, getting deeper than I would've thought possible. He repeats the action again and again and then shouts something in Russian and comes. Reaching between us, he rubs my clit with his thumb and the rest of my climax tumbles out, my muscles spasming around his thick cock, milking the rest of his seed into the condom.

"Oh my *gawd*," I pant, rocking slowly over his cock, arching my breasts toward his face each time.

"You broke the rule." Nikolai's blue eyes are warm, his smirk sexy as hell. "No spin class for you."

I stop rocking my hips and open my mouth wide in protest.

He gives the side of my ass a light slap. "I *am* mean."

"No spin class ever or just not this afternoon?"

"Depends, Freckles. You're going to have to show me how good a girl you can be."

I pull a pout. "Maybe I didn't want to be a good girl."

He chuckles and lifts me off his lap. "That's what I suspected." He removes the condom and gets up. I reach for my clothes, but he stops me with a sharp, "Clothes stay off" as he walks to the bathroom to throw the condom away.

"What if I get cold?"

"You won't be. Come here, little bunny." He takes my hand and leads me to the end of the couch, where he pushes my torso down.

"Wait, no—" I say when I realize what he intends, but it's too late. His hand cracks down on my bare ass with a resounding slap.

"Ouch!" I squeal.

He doesn't stop. He delivers a dozen or so swift slaps while I dance in place then stops and rubs my ass. "Is that what you wanted, Freckles?"

"No," I sulk, even though it is. The sting of his slaps is already morphing to heat and tingling between my legs.

"You're lying." He spanks me a few more times.

I laugh out an "ow" and rise up on my tiptoes, relieved when he stops once more to massage away the sting.

He leans down and bites the side of my waist. "You're so damn cute." He gives me one more slap. "Let's make dinner. You can put my shirt on, but only my shirt. I can't wait to see how you plan to use all those groceries."

13

Nikolai

"Slice these for the olive and caper sauce," Chelle instructs, spilling a handful of olives out of a jar onto the cutting board.

I pull a knife out the drawer and start. "I don't even know what that means," I admit. "How many slices?"

"What?"

"How many slices? To each olive?"

She laughs. "I don't know—as many as you can get. It doesn't really matter." She moves around my kitchen swiftly, grabbing things from the refrigerator, turning on the oven.

I savor the way it feels to have her here.

Kitchens are the heart of a home. Our mother showed love from the kitchen. Upstairs, in the penthouse, the kitchen is the hub of the suite. It's where everyone gathers, where our lives intersect in a non-bratva way.

And that's still true, but the way I felt about it had changed after Dima left. After everyone but me had coupled up.

It had become a place I avoided rather than gravitated to.

But now my kitchen has that feel. Not that alienating one. The feeling of home.

Chelle may be small, but she's a powerful force of nature. She fills space with her personality.

I want to renegotiate our deal. Make her stay for longer. To agree to move in and brighten my kitchen for the rest of her life.

"We need some music," she tells me.

Despite already orgasming twice today, my dick gets hard again, remembering the way she danced in her bra and panties at her house.

I turn on my speakers and pick up her phone. "Do you have a playlist on here you like?"

Her smile nearly drops me to the floor. Wide. Generous. Grateful. "Let me see it." She holds her hand out.

Rather than offer it to her, I step up right beside her, putting an arm behind her back and holding the screen out for her to unlock the phone and pull up her playlist. "Thank you," I say when she's found it, and go to her settings to sync. "Also, I know your passcode now."

It's guilt that makes me tell her. She doesn't know I spied on her in her own kitchen. That I had Dima do the full-stalker package on her. She at least ought to know that I'm the kind of guy who memorizes passwords when they're used in front of me.

She shoots me a look across the kitchen, but the music has already started, and I can see it take hold of her. There's a little nod to her head. A tiny bounce to her shoulders. "Should I be worried?" She grates the rind from a lemon onto a small plate.

"Probably," I tell her, returning to my job at the chopping board. "My brother is one of Russia's best hackers. I tend to assume any information is my business since I can get to it."

"Dima?"

I like that she remembered his name. I slice all the olives and scoop them into a small bowl for her.

"Dima. He's the most dangerous of us all in his quiet way."

She appears interested. "So, could he hack into, like, my email?" She slices the bare lemon in half and squeezes the juice into a measuring cup.

I make a scoffing sound. "In about five minutes' time."

"Is that how you knew about my dad?"

I don't particularly want to discuss this, but she deserves the truth. "From digital research, yes."

"That's… creepy." I watch a shiver run down her spine. "Just how organized is your organization?"

"I won't discuss it with you, remember?"

She absorbs this. "I guess I just… well, it seems bigger than what I thought before. I should've put it together with this building and everything."

I change the subject. "So, what's the deal with your mom? Why isn't she here helping you with Zane?" I knew from Dima's research her mom was remarried and lives in Dallas but nothing else about her.

She rolls her eyes. "My mom doesn't care about anyone but herself."

"I'm sorry."

She shrugs. "It is what it is. She left us when I was ten and Zane was six. She remarried and moved to Texas. End of story."

It suddenly makes sense to me why Chelle is so determined to take on the world by herself. She hasn't been able to rely on the people in her life who should've had her back.

I experience a fierce need to be the guy she can count on, but even as the desire fills me, I know she wouldn't accept it. She doesn't want me, and she doesn't trust me. She only wanted sex if it fulfilled a bargain.

"What can I do now?" I ask.

"Pull the bag of spinach, grapes, and red onion from the refrigerator for the salad."

"These go together?" I pull out the ingredients and a mixing bowl.

She eyes it distastefully. "You don't have a salad bowl?"

"I just moved in, remember? You can order me one of those, too."

This earns me a smile. "Yeah, you need a lot of stuff for the kitchen."

"Whatever you need," I tell her.

She shoots me a look I can't quite decipher, but her phone rings, interrupting our music. She stiffens when she sees the screen, which makes a violent streak of awareness course through my body.

"Hey Zane."

I force my fists to unclench. It's just her brother. No one to kill.

Zane's talking loud enough for me to hear through her phone. "Where are you?"

"Why?"

"Where are you, Chelle? You have to tell me."

"What's going on, Zane?" She turns her back to me, which bothers me more than I care to admit.

"I need to know where you are."

"I'm at Nikolai's. What's your deal?"

"At his apartment?"

"Yes. His very lovely apartment. We're making dinner

146

—chicken with capers and olives. I'm fine. Everything is fine," she says firmly. "I told you not to worry about me."

Either Zane goes silent, or he's speaking too quietly for me to overhear now.

No, he was silent because I hear him mutter something I can't understand, and then she holds the phone away from her ear to look at the screen and shakes her head.

She turns back and meets my eye. "Zane has lost his mind."

"What is it?" I'm on edge. There's a prickle of warning running up my spine, but I don't know how to interpret it. Chelle isn't in danger from her brother.

Maybe I am.

Well, that's fine. I can handle Zane, so long as I see him coming. He can't get in the building without my permission, and I'm protected at the games. He won't know where else to find me, unless Chelle tips him off.

"I don't know. He was demanding to know where I was. And then he cursed and hung up."

"He may want to kill me," I say it mildly, but her eyes go round and wide. She looks back at her phone, then her thumbs start flying over her screen as she texts him something.

I decide not to be a dick and ask to see it.

The oven alarm goes off, and she startles, then pulls the chicken out using a dishrag. "You need hot mitts," she tells me as she sets the tray on top of the stove.

"Order whatever you like," I tell her again. She bustles around putting the rest of the dinner together, looking tense and unhappy.

I set the table and help with the salad. "Hey." I rest my hands lightly on her waist from behind. "Don't worry about Zane. I'll handle him."

She nods but doesn't turn around.

I want to fix it, but I can't. I'm the one who chose to use someone's sister to pay off his debt. The deal was rotten from the start. Of course, we'll all suffer the repercussions.

14

Chelle

After dinner, Nikolai tells me to put some clothes on.

"Are we going somewhere?"

"Yes. Down to the lake, so dress warmly."

Warmth and something else—excitement, maybe—ricochet through me. I go to his bedroom to put on a pair of jeans and a warm sweater. This shouldn't be so fun. Playing house with Nikolai.

The sex. Making dinner together. Now a walk by the lake. It feels romantic and sweet. Like he's my boyfriend, not a guy I sold my body and soul to for the next month.

Is he trying to... woo me?

No, that's ridiculous. Why would he? Except when I review everything that's passed between us until now through that lens, it almost fits.

He took me home from the Red Room but refused to have sex with me. Like a gentleman. He wouldn't take my car. Also, very gallant. He let me have the ring back with the payment of a single kiss. He came out to dinner with me—which was a huge favor for me to ask, considering we had no relationship. And then he wanted to be invited up.

That's the single most damning piece of evidence I have.

He wanted to be invited up, but I refused, which seemed to hurt him. And then he offered me this deal.

My pulse races as I consider all these facts.

Does Nikolai actually *like me?*

For more than sex?

The idea thrills me, even as I throw up a dozen barriers around my heart. I can't get involved with Nikolai.

As amazing as the sex is, and as much as he fascinates me, I would never, ever date a guy in the Russian *mafiya*.

I mean, never, ever, ever.

It was bad enough my dad was a gambler, but at least that was legal. I could never align myself with someone who does things that aren't. Someone who operates from violence.

No. Nikolai is a dangerous man in an even more dangerous organization.

There's no way I can even consider getting excited over the fact that he might like me.

Of course, the flutters and warmth zooming around in my chest don't wait for permission to exist. I can't control my way out of my own attraction to Nikolai.

I grab my jacket and emerge from the bedroom. When I pick up my purse, Nikolai takes it off my shoulder and sets it down. "You won't need that." He takes my hand. "Let's go."

I try to shut down the flutters as we take the elevator to the ground floor, but they refuse to obey. My body is alive at Nikolai's nearness. My nerve endings tingling to be close to him. To breathe the faint scent of his soap and aftershave.

We get off on the ground floor and walk out to the lobby. The same tattooed guy is at the front desk as the first time I came to the Kremlin.

"Do you ever get an hour off around here?" I pretend we're friendly, and I didn't cry and beg and climb him like a tree last time I saw him.

He grins. "My shift just started." His gaze flicks between me and Nikolai with interest. "I'm Maykl."

Nikolai growls something in Russian, and he wipes the smile off his face.

"I'm Chelle." I hold my hand out.

Maykl glances at Nikolai without reaching for it.

"What did you say?" I demand.

"I told him not to flirt with you or his tongue would end up like Oleg's," Nikolai mutters.

My smile grows wider, and I extend my hand further. "You can shake my hand," I tell Maykl. "Nikolai already owns me."

Nikolai's chuckle sounds involuntary.

As soon as Maykl sees the smile, he clasps my hand and squeezes too hard.

"Ow." I wiggle my fingers when he releases it. "You're stronger than you think."

"Show off," Nikolai growls. "Touch her again, and you die."

I can't stop the cascade of pleasure that runs through me at Nikolai's possessiveness. I was right.

He likes me.

I grasp his elbow like we're on a formal date and smile up at him as he leads me out of the glass doors and onto the sidewalk.

His return smile is warm. He winks, and I beam like a lunatic. "Don't ever climb him again," he says, and I burst into laughter.

"You didn't like that? I was trying to see you."

"You were trying to get your ring back," he grumbles.

"You got a kiss out of it," I remind him, and his fond smile returns. "And some light groping, which pretty much rocked my world, I must confess."

Now I get teeth with the smile. Nikolai stops and yanks my body up against his, looping his arm around my back. I lose my breath, tipping my face up to his. His hand wanders to my ass like it did during that kiss. "Let's have a repeat, then," he murmurs as he lowers his lips to mine.

It's dark out, and the sidewalk is mostly empty. His body blocks the chilly wind coming off the lake, and his breath is warm on my face. He strokes his lips over mine softly once. I'm instantly on fire, my body now fully belonging to him. I reach for his face and kiss him back, my tongue prying his lips apart. He squeezes and kneads my ass with one hand, then adds the other. I loop my hands around his neck and jump to straddle him.

He chuckles against my lips.

"Can I climb you, then?"

"Right where I want you," he declares and kisses me until I grow dizzy.

Voices sound from behind him, and he sets me back down with a groan. "Tomorrow I won't let you leave my bed for even a minute."

"Aw, come on." I loop my arm through his again. "You have me all month."

His smile fades and some of the warmth leaves his eyes. He looks ahead instead of down at me as we walk and my stomach tightens.

Nikolai wants more than this arrangement.

I'd already figured that out before we came downstairs, but his change in mood drove it home.

152

I should tell him now—explain why I can't do this for real.

Except I can't bring myself to speak. I don't want to say the words. To further ruin what was a magical moment.

When we get to the water's edge, Nikolai stops at a rack of bicycles for rent and takes out his credit card.

"What are you doing?" I demand.

"You missed your spin class. I thought we could go for a ride along the lake shore."

"Oh, no. We can't! I'm not a street rider," I say immediately.

He raises a brow as he completes the transaction for the first bike. "I don't get it."

"I mean, riding outside where there are people and laws you have to follow is a totally different thing. It would be dangerous."

He lowers the seat on the bike he unlocked and turns on the headlight. "I'll keep you safe," he promises, as if the danger would be from someone attacking us, and not me running into a pole, or falling on my head. He pushes the bike toward me, and I reluctantly take charge of it.

"I can't ride a bike in the dark!" I protest.

"Of course you can. Trust me, *zayka*. It will be fun." He finishes unlocking the second bike and throws his leg over it. "Come on, we'll go slowly." He turns on his headlight.

"We don't have helmets!"

"Chelle." He says my name so quietly, it has the effect of settling me and capturing my attention. He holds my gaze. "It will be fun."

I have no choice but to believe him. I mount the bike and start pedaling, controlling the wobble beneath me.

Nikolai passes me, a broad grin on his face. "Keep up, Freckles," he calls over his shoulder.

"Oh, it's on," I retort, pushing hard into my pedals to catch up.

Nikolai's chuckle carries on the wind, and I pull up beside him. He leads me to the sidewalk that runs along the lake shore. During the day, it's usually packed with people, but at this time of night, there's no one out here. We have the whole walkway to ourselves. The clouds part, revealing a bright white moon that creates a long, continuous reflection on the water.

As my anxiety over hitting someone or falling in the dark ebbs, the perfection of it all seeps in. The wind on my face and in my hair. Nikolai's laughter. The sensation of speed, the beauty of the lake.

My body turns on. There's nothing sexual about it, but physical pleasure overtakes me, just the same. I grind over the bicycle seat like it's my vibrator, increasing the sensations.

"You were right," I call to Nikolai, laughter in my voice.

He throws me a smile. "You're having fun?"

"So much."

It's true. I can't think of when I've felt so free. So joyous. I never let myself go. I have to control every aspect of my life, right down to when and how I could have sex with Nikolai.

This bike ride? It's freedom.

Freedom from constraint. From my crazy mind trying to make everything work out perfect and tie up with a bow, which it never does.

Nikolai is showing me something so much bigger than a bike ride along the lake. Something about living.

About love.

Wait, no. No, no, no. I'm not in love.

I can't fall in love.

Yet, even as my mind protests, my body's sailing free. Exalting in the sensations of the joyous bike ride.

In partnership with the man riding beside me.

Gratitude flows to him for bringing me out here. Showing me this. Making me come out of the safety of my controls and limitations.

I grind down on the seat again, letting myself turn completely untethered. Masturbating on a bike seat in the moonlight.

I come. Not a big orgasm. More like a little ripple, but it feels like a symbol of success. I let go and nothing terrible happened. There was actually a reward.

15

Nikolai

After morning sex and Chelle's champagne brunch Sunday, I feel like a king.

No, more like I've been reborn. For the last four years, my bratva cell was my entire world. Ravil was the most benevolent dictator—all-seeing, generous, inclusive. Living all together on the top floor of this building was everything to me.

When things changed, I lost my way. My identity. What to live for.

Now, with this place, with Chelle running around naked doing my bidding, I feel like life restarted.

"Come here, Freckles." I slide out and turn one of the barstools at the breakfast bar around. "Climb up here." I pat it.

She comes over, her nipples beaded up and perky. I grasp her waist and lift her onto the bar stool.

"Good girl."

Her gaze is both interested and wary. She trusts me,

though. More and more. And I fucking love the way that trust feels.

I'd been lost before she came here. Empty. Feeling like I had no real purpose in life. Now I've found it. It's turning Chelle on. Earning her trust. Watching her bloom like the most exotic, delicate flower.

I pick up a length of rope and wrap it around her calves, binding them to the legs of the barstool, so her knees are open, the sweet pink heart of her sex exposed to me. She squirms on the seat.

I catch her gaze. "Turned on?"

She nods.

"That's too bad because I'm going to make you wait for it today. Do not disobey me and come without permission this time, or there will be serious consequences."

"I don't really think I can help it," she complains.

"Then, by all means, test me," I dare and watch her throat bob as she swallows.

She looks beautiful, her chestnut hair tumbling across her shoulders, her face flushed, pretty lips parted. Her tongue darts out to lick them, and I have to rearrange my package.

I wind the rope around her ribs and waist, binding her to the seat back, but leaving her breasts free for me to play with. "Give me your wrists," I command from behind her. She hesitates, then holds her arms behind her for me to grasp and behind together.

I walk around to the front of her and survey my work.

It's fucking deadly.

I mean, she's so hot the apartment is in danger of combusting.

I pull out my phone to snap a picture, and she freaks out.

"Hard limit!" she yelps immediately, jerking at the bonds. "No photos. I mean it, Nikolai."

"Okay, Freckles." I toss my phone on the counter to calm her down. "I would never share it, is that what you're afraid of?"

"Hard limit," is all she can say, but the depth of her reaction makes me think there's more to it.

"Hm." I saunter toward her and put a knuckle under her chin to lift it. "What happened?"

She struggles against the bonds again, and I slide my hand under her hair to cup her nape. "Easy, Freckles. I don't want you to chafe." I stare down at her, massaging her neck and waiting until her breath deepens. "You're quite obviously at my mercy here." I pick up the bottle of peppermint oil I bought for the occasion and dab a bit on each of her nipples, then swirl it around to rub it in.

She blinks at me, then drags her lower lip between her teeth with a hiss when the burn starts to set in.

"I asked you a question." I keep my tone casual and conversational, circling her without letting my fingertips stray from her body.

She squirms in her seat.

"There's a story behind the photos, I can tell."

Her belly puffs out and sucks in on a deep breath. "How can you tell?"

I smile. "Don't answer a question with a question, *zayka*." I pinch one of her nipples and hold it tight between my fingers until she gasps. I release it. "Talk to me. I want to know what happened."

"Rob Sharke," she gasps.

I stand in front of her and slide my hands up and down her thighs, squeezing every now and then.

"He shared photos of you?"

She nods. "He was my boyfriend in high school. Well, I

159

thought he was my boyfriend. He was just trying to get laid
—a total player. He took me to senior prom. I had sex with
him." She shrugs. "He broke up with me the following
week."

Now I understand why she hates players. I hate that
she bundled me with such an asshole, but I get it. This is
why she had to be roped into sex with a contract and a
deadline. She's afraid to give it freely now because it was
taken in bad faith before.

I feel the spark of vengeance kindle in my gut. The
need to hurt the asshole for her. "And the photos?" There's
a dangerous edge to my voice.

She nods. "You guessed it. The next summer I found
out all the guys from high school had been privy to them.
At least I'd already graduated, but I've never felt so
violated."

I straighten. "Tell me where to find him, and I'll break
both his arms."

She lets out a disbelieving laugh. "You're crazy."

"Perfectly sane. And very dangerous when truly
angered. Give me a name, and he'll pay for his crimes
against you."

She shakes her head. "That's wrong, Nikolai." Even so,
I can tell she likes it. There's a smile still playing around
the corners of her mouth and ease returns to her body.

"Offer stands." I return to tweaking her nipples. Then
I pick up the little bullet vibrator I also bought and slide it
between her legs. I move slowly, making her watch it and
wriggle in anticipation. I tuck it between her nether lips,
flush against her clit and she moans.

"You like that, little bunny?"

She moans louder.

I hold her throat lightly, tracing my thumb down the
front of it. "Answer my question, *zayka*."

"Yes."

"Good." I leave her that way and walk behind her, out of her line of sight.

"Nikolai?"

I don't answer.

"Wait, what are you doing?" A thread of panic rings in her voice.

"Letting you simmer," I reply. "Remember that you don't have permission to come."

"Oh my God," she moans. "This is crazy. You can't do this to me. Nikolai?"

"Be good," I warn.

I leave to wash my hands with soap to make sure the peppermint oil is gone before I move to the next stage of my plan. I put on her favorite song, "Low," or at least the one she danced to in her kitchen because it has now become my favorite.

When I walk around to the front of her, she's in a semi-trance like state, her head lolling, her eyes dilated. She rolls her hips slowly forward and back over the vibrator, looking like the most beautiful eye candy I've ever seen.

"*Blyad,*' Chelle." I give my dick a hard squeeze over my jeans. "I can't wait to fuck you."

She straightens her spine. "Then do it." Her voice has a pleading quality. She squirms against the ropes. "Please, Nikolai."

I'm convinced.

I walk behind her and start to untie her wrists. "I'm not going to fuck that tight little pussy of yours this time," I warn her.

"Oh God," she murmurs.

I grasp her throat from behind and bring my lips to her ear. "You ready to get your ass fucked by me?"

She whimpers.

"I think you are." I pause in my untying. "Or do you need more time with the vibrator?"

"No," she says quickly, then backpedals. "I mean, I don't know... "

I chuckle. "You liked it last night when I fucked you with the plug."

"You are *so dirty*," she says like she's offended, except I hear levity in her voice.

"You like it dirty," I counter. I get her hands untied and work on her torso. The ropes were fun, and she looked beautiful, but now I can't get them off her fast enough. "Next time I'm going to tie you in a position I can fuck you in," I mutter and she laughs.

I free her completely, but hold her in place when she starts to jump down from the barstool. "Uh uh." I push the bullet vibe inside her, still running, then heft her over my shoulder.

"Oh my God, Nikolai!" she giggles as I walk her to the bedroom. I give her ass a slap before I drop her in the middle of the bed.

"On your knees and elbows, *zayka*," I command.

She rolls over and climbs into position.

I curse in Russian because she looks so hot. The vibrator hums between her legs, making her pussy leak with juices. Grabbing the lubricant, I apply a generous amount to her anus then to my cock.

She doesn't resist this time. Humming softly, she pushes back to take me, and I press forward. She lets out a wanton cry—half pain, half pleasure as my head passes through the tight ring of muscles.

"Nikolai," she sobs.

I go slowly, feeding her inch by inch until my cock is fully seated. I wait, watching her bowed back move with her pants. When she sags a little, I begin to slowly pump.

She lets out a cry with each movement, but I hear the satisfaction in her notes. She grows louder with each one, throwing my name in every once in a while.

"You can touch yourself, *zayka*."

"Ohhhhhh," she moans as she reaches between her legs to rub her clit. "Nikolai, may I please come?"

I curse again in Russian, my balls drawing up. She's so fucking sweet. "Da," I grunt. "Come, little bunny."

I grip her hips and pound in faster, taking care not to be too rough.

Her moans and shrieks send me over the edge, and I thrust in harder and faster, lights dancing in front of my eyes.

"Come, Chelle," I croak right before I hurtle across the finish line. I squeeze the sides of her ass too tight, giving her short little thrusts as I come and come like I'll never stop.

When I finish, I reach underneath her hips to help. "Did you come?" I ask hoarsely, rubbing her clit.

She cries out, and her entire pelvic floor tightens and draws up, squeezing my dick more than I would've thought possible. She moans and moans as it rolls through her, and I rub her clit the whole time. As soon as she goes still, I ease out.

"Nikolai," she gasps. I love hearing my name in that torn, raspy voice. "Oh my God."

I kiss her shoulder and tug the bullet vibe out. She collapses on the bed like I melted her bones. I wash up in the bathroom and bring a washcloth to clean her.

"Mmm," she hums softly.

"Worth it," I mutter to myself.

She rolls to her back, her small breasts separating, her nipples still stiff. "What is?"

"You."

Her gaze meets mine, and she's not my little fire-cracker. She looks vulnerable, like she wants to believe me, but is afraid there's some trick.

I palm her breast and lean over to give her a slow, open-mouthed kiss. I want to tell her she can trust me. That we won't break up now that we've had sex, but I realize it's irrelevant. I can't heal her wounds if she doesn't want me. And Chelle's never going to accept what I am. Who I am.

16

Nikolai

Mid-week, I get a call from the guy named Viper. I'm upstairs in the penthouse, and the moment I get it, I signal to Sasha to silence the television, and I point to the phone. Maxim and Ravil walk over, and I put the guy on speaker.

"Heard you were in the market for pussy."

"That's right. To own not rent," I answer.

"Who do you work for?"

"My boss is head of the Chicago bratva," I tell him. "Are your girls Russian?"

"Yes. Which is a problem, since none of us speak Russian."

My nostrils flare as I meet Ravil's cold gaze.

"My boss has resources." Meaning—we can afford to buy the women.

"I'll deal with him directly."

"He's right here." I hand Ravil the phone.

"Ravil Baranov. Who am I speaking with?"

"You can call me Viper. How many girls do you want?"

Ravil sends us all a grim look. "How many are available?"

"Fourteen."

"How much?"

"Two thousand a piece."

A choking sound beside me reminds me that Sasha's in the room. She has one hand clapped over her mouth, and her big, expressive eyes swim with tears. Maxim reaches out and squeezes her shoulder.

"I'll give you twenty-five thousand for the lot."

A shocked scoffing sound emits from under Sasha's hand.

"All right. You have the money now?"

"I have it."

"Tonight. Eleven-thirty. I'll text an address at eleven." He ends the call without a goodbye.

"What. The holy fuck?" Sasha cries. "I'm going to puke."

"You shouldn't have heard that." Maxim sends a glare my way.

"Apologies. I shouldn't have taken the call in here."

"No, you shouldn't have," Ravil agrees. "Times have changed. We have women and children in the penthouse. No business anywhere but my office from now on."

"Understood," I agree.

"You're not… you're going to set them free, aren't you?" Sasha asks.

"Of course we are," Maxim says. "We're trying to get to their source." He looks at Ravil. "I can't believe how little they're selling them for."

"I can," Ravil says grimly. "The global reach of human trafficking has sent the price to a rock-bottom low."

"Are these the same people who took Nadia?" Sasha guesses.

Ravil shrugs. "There might be a connection.."

"Are we telling Adrian?" I ask.

Ravil considers for a moment. "Yes. Loop him in. We'll bring a crowd." He looks at Maxim. "Put together a team."

~

I LEAVE my beautiful sex slave well-sated in bed at ten-thirty.

"Where are you going?" she murmurs sleepily.

I strap an extra holster to my calf and check my weapon, which makes her sit up with a frown between her brows.

"Go to sleep, Freckles. I have business to take care of."

"What kind of business?" I hear a tautness in her voice and wish to hell I'd waited until she was fully asleep before I got up.

"Don't ask me questions about business, Chelle. It's a rule." When her frown deepens to a scowl, I add, "It's for your own safety and protection."

She curls back on her side to watch me, a line firmly etched between her brows.

I lean over and try to kiss it away. "Stop thinking so hard—this doesn't concern you. Go to sleep."

She doesn't answer, and I know we just took five steps back from the progress we'd made toward her accepting me.

Well, fuck. This is what I am. I can't change it or help it. I knew she couldn't hang with it long term, and to expect any differently would be delusional.

I meet the guys on the sixth floor where we have a lounge for the soldiers lower in the ranks. There are sixteen of us in all, and Maxim has assigned us one or two to a vehicle, with extra SUVs along to transport the women, presuming all goes well. Dima is on video conference with us and Ravil is here, but Maxim won't let him come along. Ever since his son was born, we've protected our *pakhan* from the most dangerous activities. The idea of him being taken from his baby is too much for any of us to bear, especially his wife, Lucy.

"This is an information gathering mission," Maxim says firmly. "We are bringing you all for protection not to exterminate. Our objective is to get the women out safely and find out who is behind the operation." He gives Adrian a sharp look. "Understood?"

There are a chorus of yeses and *da*s, but Adrian remains stony-faced.

"Adrian, did you hear me? This is our chance to find out if Poval's behind this and where he might be. If you fuck this up, we lose the lead." Maxim raises his brows.

Adrian scowls.

"I need to hear your acknowledgement."

"I understand," Adrian says with obvious reluctance. I don't blame him. I wouldn't mind killing all these fuckers, either.

I receive the text with the address just after eleven and read it out loud. Dima instantly pulls up a map of a warehouse and sends the pin to all the drivers.

"Let's move out," Maxim orders, and we file out to take the elevator to the underground parking garage.

I ride with Oleg, Adrian and Maxim. Oleg drives. At the warehouse, we take the lead, the rest of the guys spreading out to cover our backs. Maxim has the cash in a bag.

We're greeted at the door by two guys with machine guns. They allow only Maxim and I to come inside and insist we drop our weapons into a crate, which doesn't surprise me. I try leaving the Glock at my ankle, but the guy who pats me down finds it and takes it away.

Maxim and I play it cool, even though our lives are at risk.

Inside, a group of women are tethered together like a chain-gang, surrounded by lethal-looking men with machine guns. We're in an empty warehouse. I'm guessing this location was picked for the transaction not because it has any meaning to their operation.

A muscle in Maxim's jaw flexes. He tosses the bag of cash onto the floor in front of us.

Rattlesnake steps forward to pick it up and count it, then he nods at a man standing back, puffing on a cigar. Like Rattlesnake, he has serpent tattoos crawling up his neck. "It all there?" he asks.

"Yeah. It's good."

One of the women makes eye contact with me. She looks malnourished and scared.

"It's all right," I murmur in Russian, and she goes still, like she understands me.

"Yeah, I figure you'll have better use for them," the man I presume is Viper says. "Them not understanding got old fast."

"You have more than these?" Maxim asks.

The guy shrugs. "No more to sell."

"Where did they come from?"

"I came into them," he says, then looks at Rattlesnake. "Unlock the chains."

"Let's go," I say in Russian to the women as Rattlesnake unlocks their ankle chains. "You're safe now. You're free."

The women bolt for the door, the moment they get free of the chains, and Maxim and I wait. My hands are clammy, and my stomach is sick over the deal, but I don't let any of that show on my face. We pause until all the women are free and then walk out, picking our weapons up from the crate when we get outside.

The women, who are in bare feet and barely enough clothing to cover them, have scattered, some sprinting away, some running for the warmth and shelter of our cars.

Adrian and the other soldiers shout after them in Russian, promising them safety and freedom, being careful not to chase or spook them, and eventually they all get in.

"*Fuck*," Maxim says when we climb into Oleg's SUV.

Adrian won't get in, even though everyone else has driven off.

"We can't go in, Adrian. They have machine guns," I say, knowing what he's thinking. "Get in the SUV."

Still, Adrian stands there.

"They're not getting a pass, we're just biding our time. Get in the fucking car," Maxim says. "That's an order."

Adrian turns and stalks back, a deep line between his brows. He climbs in and slams the door, his face murderous.

"We'll take them down," I promise.

"Yes, we will," Maxim affirms. "Every last one of them. And when we find Poval, you can make him pay."

Adrian sits back, his upper lip curling. "His death *will not* be swift," he vows darkly.

17

Chelle

I run my fingertip over the gunshot wound on the side of Nikolai's abdomen, and he catches my wrist. We're in bed on Wednesday morning. I should get up and get ready for work, but he just left me so sated, I can't move, nor do I want to.

I've been Nikolai's sex slave for a week and a half now.

It seems like I should hate it. I should hate everything about this. I'm using my body to pay off a sizable debt to the mob. Nikolai literally owns me and can make me do pretty much anything he wants or the deal is off.

Instead, it feels like glorious fantasy fulfillment.

I love that our arrangement has a start and end date. That the rules are very well defined. Nikolai gives me assignments or tells me what he wants, and I obey. It's like a job, and it seems to be one I'm good at, based on the boss' constant hard-on for me.

Of course, he makes it fun. The things he demands of me are always a turn-on. He's not hurting me or making me do things I hate. Just pushing my boundaries a little.

I've tried to ask about the scar before, but he doesn't want to talk about it. Probably because it involves a crime.

That scares the crap out of me. I don't even know what I'm afraid of. His getting shot again? Getting caught for a crime he committed? Finding out he's done things that will yank me out of this little fantasy world?

"Does it hurt?"

"No. But I don't like the way it feels." Nikolai's tone warns me not to go on.

"When did it happen? May I ask?"

At my second question, Nikolai's face softens into his signature smirk. "No, you may not ask. I told you that already."

"Because you were doing something illegal?" I can't stop myself from pushing. It's like the car crash you can't look away from.

"No, I don't like the way you get either scared or judgy about these things."

My eyes widen, and his words hit me square in the chest. I realize it's the first time he's criticized anything about me, and I hate the way it feels.

"About what things?" My voice comes out sounding hoarse.

He shrugs. "About what I do. Or what you think I do." He rolls off the bed and gets up.

He's usually the one focused on me. I didn't realize how addictive that attention was until he withdrew it.

I'm left cold. This is how it will feel when our month is over. When he's through with me. Just like Rob Sharke. But that's wrong. The end date was something I appreciate about our arrangement. Being hurt when it's over would be absurd. I wouldn't want this thing to go on indefinitely.

And making Nikolai's withdrawal about me when he's clearly the hurt party is even more ridiculous. I get out of bed and follow him, wrapping my arms around his waist from behind. He holds my hands and turns to face me. There's surprise etched on his face, and for some reason, that adds to my guilt.

Like I haven't shown him any affection when he's been nothing but a gentleman with me. A very dirty and demanding gentleman but always considerate.

"I wasn't asking to know more about what you do, I was asking to know more about *you*," I try to explain.

He cocks a brow.

"You don't share that much. I mean about the inner Nikolai. You hold your cards close to the vest."

"Do you play poker, Chelle?"

I realize this is how he deflects. Asking me questions and never answering any of mine.

"My dad taught us both. Zane is better at it than I am."

Nikolai nods. "Zane's a good player."

"Do you play?" I realize I know nothing about how his games even work. "Or are you the dealer?"

"No to both questions. I watch."

"You facilitate."

"Yes."

I think of how well he handled my crazy skateboarding clients. "You're good at that."

Both his brows shoot up in surprise. His arms circle my waist, wrapped over the top of mine and he pulls me closer. "How do you know?" I love the seductive rumble in his voice.

"Because you're the perfect manager. You manage people without them knowing they're being handled. Like my clients. And…" I realize it's true as the thought hits me. "Me."

Nikolai presses a kiss to the top of my head. "Hmm."

I wait, hoping for once, he'll share more.

"Sometimes I think I'm good at nothing. I have no special skill. Not like Dima. I just break noses and collect money, and I'm not even the guy who's good at that. I bring Oleg and Adrian along to do my dirty work."

"That's what I mean. You're the manager. *You* are the special skill. Who you are."

Nikolai searches my face like there's some answer there he wants to believe.

"You could do anything and be successful at it. You're a natural facilitator." I'm sure of the words the moment they come out of my mouth. I'd been nervous bringing him along to that dinner, but he'd shone. Now that I know him, I'm almost certain I'd want him on my team for most any activity.

Nikolai cradles the side of my face in his hand and leans down to brush his lips across mine. "You're sweet, Chelle Goldberg."

"I'm not being sweet, I'm telling you my honest opinion."

"Well, that honest opinion just earned you a visit to the Red Room tonight. Accompanied by me, of course."

I kiss him hard. "You are the best. I promise I won't let any random guys buy me a drink."

"I wouldn't let that happen, bunny rabbit. I would kill them first."

I steal a glance at his face to see if he's joking. His eyes twinkle, so I think he is, but this is a guy with a bullet hole through his gut, so I can't be entirely sure.

He turns me toward the bathroom and slaps my ass. "You'd better get a move on, or you'll be late for work, Ms. Junior Publicist."

I laugh and scoot to the shower, loving how staying

here with Nikolai is both magical and easy. I'm simultaneously comfortable with and excited by him at all times.

Sounds like love, a little voice in my head sings.

But that can't be right. I can't be falling in love with Nikolai.

Guys with bullet holes aren't keepers.

Even if they do make your heart sing.

Nikolai

I love taking Chelle to the Red Room. We haven't been out together, other than our bicycle rides around the lakeshore or shopping, and I enjoy the thought of spoiling her. Or maybe I just like the idea of fitting into her life. As strange as that dinner with Skate 32 had been, I liked seeing a glimpse of her life. How she thinks when she works. Now I get to see how she plays.

"Well, hello, you two," her girlfriend Shanna greets us when we arrive, sliding a cocktail napkin across the bar in front of each of us.

"Nikolai, this is Shanna. I think you sort of met last time."

"We did." I put my hand out to shake hers.

"He was mad at me for trying to help you get laid. But it looks like it all worked out in the end, right?" She winks at Chelle, who blushes a pretty pink.

"Don't meddle in my sex life if you don't want me to meddle in yours." Chelle shoots a pointed look at the other bartender—a tattooed guy in his mid-thirties who looks like he's doing inventory at the other end of the bar.

"Stop it," Shanna says immediately.

I drag Chelle's barstool closer to my side and drape an

arm behind her back. "What are you drinking? Dirty martini?"

She blinks at me in surprise. "You really pay attention, don't you?"

"I've got her, what would you like?" Shanna asks.

"Grey Goose, neat."

"Aw, come on, Russian stereotype. You really drink straight vodka?" She gives me a look of disbelief, then shrugs. "Okay."

"I can have a beer if it makes you feel better."

"Nope. No. I'm actually loving it." Shanna pours and serves the drinks without even looking at what she's doing, clearly comfortable behind the bar. She sets them down in front of us. "So why are you here? I thought you'd be home, you know—getting your money's worth." She waggles her brows at me as Chelle blushes again.

I look at Chelle, amused. "You told her, her?"

"I'm sorry. Is that bad? I had to tell someone."

"I don't kiss and tell, but I think it's different for women."

"Yep. We kiss and tell all over the place," Shanna says loudly, right as the other bartender walks behind her.

His step hitches. "Who did you kiss?"

"Not me, her," Shanna jerks her thumb at Chelle, but she turns her body to fully face the other bartender, a flirty smirk on her face.

He stares at her for a moment then seems to shake himself and looks our way. "Hey, Chelle."

"Hi, Derek. This is Nikolai, my, um…"

"Your kiss and tell?" Derek asks, leaning across the bar to shake my hand. "Nice to meet you."

"Likewise."

"Derek owns this place," Chelle explains. To him, she

says, "Hey, Derek—Nikolai's friend has a band I think you should hear. They're great. They're called The Storytellers. They play at Rue's Lounge every Thursday. I think you should have them here."

My throat tightens. I probably shouldn't read so much into it, but Chelle's interest in my friends makes me feel like she's part of my life, too. Like she's my girlfriend not just my captive sex goddess.

"Only if you do the publicity for it," Derek throws out.

"Deal," she shoots back.

"Yeah? Cool. Have them call me on a Sunday or Monday to get it on the schedule."

"Great." Chelle beams, and I squeeze her shoulder. After Derek walks away, she says, "I don't even know if they'd want to play here, but I thought it would be fun." She shrugs.

"I'm sure they'd be thrilled. They're always looking for gigs."

"I think the Skate 32's video launch could be their big break. They have a huge following. It might get them some play beyond Chicago, you know?"

"Maybe they should hire you as their publicist." I smile.

"They probably couldn't afford Image First, but I'm happy to help out pro bono for now."

"You never know what they could afford. Oleg has money, and Story is his reason for living."

Chelle's face goes soft and dreamy, and I can't stop myself from leaning forward to kiss her.

When I pull away, her eyes are closed, dark lashes fanning over her freckled cheeks. I steal another kiss. "You're beautiful," I murmur.

She blinks at me like she's surprised.

Like no one's ever told her that before.

I want to promise her everything. That I'll keep calling her beautiful every day until she learns to expect it. That I'll be her man.

But she doesn't want a man. At least, not a man like me.

18

Nikolai

I sit in my Tesla in front of Chelle's spin class.

She's been a perfect angel for the two and a half weeks I've owned her. I've used and abused her body in as many dirty ways as I can think of, and the more I do, the softer she gets.

So when she asked me over breakfast this morning if she could go to her spin class, I felt like only a *mudak* would say no.

But I didn't want to let the leash out too long, so I'm here to pick her up. Maybe take her out to dinner. She's cooked for me all week. Not always fancy like the first night and her Sunday brunches, but she does like to be in the kitchen, even if it's just throwing together a salad, or baking peanut butter and chocolate chip cookies.

I love having her in my kitchen. In my apartment. Turns out it wasn't the furniture that was wrong before. It was missing Chelle. Although she's right—the new thick glass dining set she found is a delight beside the big windows.

Chelle exits the building and looks around. I pull out from where I was illegally parked to pick her up right in front. She slides in the passenger seat with a broad smile. "Sorry, were you waiting long?"

"No," I lie. I came to haunt the place like a stalker almost the minute the class started.

"Would it be all right if we stopped by my apartment to pick up a few things?"

"Sure." I change lanes to head in the right direction. "Do you want to go out to eat?"

She looks down at her workout outfit, which I'd forgotten to consider when I developed my plan. "Um, yeah. If I can take a quick shower and change at my place."

"That works."

She looks over at me. "How was your day?"

I shrug. I'm not going to tell her I was contacted by and arranged a meet with Rattlesnake's boss to find out the scoop on his sex slave trade. "Uneventful. How about yours?"

"It was good. I guess the skaters are actually moving forward with using the Storyteller's music for their videos. I'm going to do some events around it, like a live video chat with the band and the skaters talking about their collaboration. I need to get in touch with Story to get all their info. I figured you would hook me up?"

"Of course," I say. "She lives upstairs."

I haven't brought Chelle up to the penthouse yet. She's not one of us, and she's not my girlfriend, either. She's just someone I'm screwing for the month. Someone who will be gone in thirteen days. A fact that makes me want to wrench the steering wheel off and throw it out my window.

I shouldn't bring her upstairs. I can't let her see anything about the bratva, including the way we live or the layout of things. We learned the hard way with Dima's girlfriend Natasha, that the FBI could use anyone to get information on us. I also don't want the guys knowing about the deal I made with her. Dima already figured it out when we talked this week, but if I can keep the rest from knowing, I will.

"I'll get her number," I tell Chelle. I don't even have it because it's not like we text each other's girlfriends, especially when we live in the same suite. I can text Oleg for it though.

We get to her place, and I walk upstairs with her. The moment we get in front of her door, I know something's wrong. The door frame appears cracked.

I grab her wrist as she stretches her hand out to unlock the door, and I yank her behind my body. Pushing the door with my toe, I watch it swing wide—locks broken. I motion for Chelle to stay in the hallway and creep forward, reaching for the Glock at the back of my waist.

Her place is trashed. Her television is gone. The kitchen drawers all stand open like they've been searched. I creep forward, listening closely for any sounds. The bedroom has also been trashed—her dresser drawers pulled out and upended, things scattered everywhere.

I search the place thoroughly before I go back out to the hallway where I find Chelle standing pale and trembling. She looks at the gun in my hand with bug eyes.

Dammit.

"Looks like a burglary. They took your TV and searched all your stuff. Probably looking for jewelry or cash. They've gone now."

"Oh God. What should we do?"

"Call your brother first."

She blinks at me. "Wh-why?"

I take her phone from her cold fingers, pull up Zane's

number, and press the call button. I hold it out to her. "Find out if he knows anything about this."

Her golden eyes grow even wider, and she lets out her breath on a small sob.

Zane answers, which I didn't expect. "Chelle?" he sounds alarmed.

I don't like it.

"Zane? My place has been trashed. They stole my TV, and I don't know what else."

"Fuck! Where are you now? Are you there? Is Nikolai with you?"

I grab the phone from Chelle's hand, a white-hot rage burning through me. "What did you do, Zane?" I snap.

"Nikolai." Zane sounds breathless. "Get my sister out of there, would you? Keep her safe."

"What in the fuck is going on?" I snarl. I am seriously going to kill that kid for doing this to Chelle.

"I, ah, I had a drug deal going on, but the shit got stolen. Now I'm into the dealer for the cost of goods."

"A drug deal with who?"

I watch Chelle mouth the word, *whom*, while her eyes stare straight forward, like she's shell-shocked and scared.

"Not your problem."

"You just made it my fucking problem when they came after Chelle," I snarl.

"You're the one who came after Chelle!" Zane thunders back. "You *took my sister*. I'm trying to buy her back, you insane fucking Russian. So just get her out of there, and I'll get you your damn money!" He ends the call before I can rip him a new one, and I hold the phone against my chest like that will somehow shield Chelle from what she just heard.

Blyad.'

Zane is right. I took his sister. I triggered all of this by bringing her into the equation. And even though this is completely consensual on her part, I made veiled threats about harming her from the beginning, so Zane's assumption of the worst is on me.

Fuckity fuck fuck.

Chelle's chin starts to shiver, and I pull her slender body against mine. "It's okay. It's going to be fine. I'll take care of your apartment. Let's get you out of here."

"Shouldn't we call the cops?"

"No. I'll replace your stuff, okay? Don't worry about any of it." I close the door as best I can, turn her around and maneuver her down the hall, still tucked tightly against my side.

"Are you going to explain to me what's happening?" Her voice quavers, and it kills me.

"Zane is trying to rescue you from me and whatever he did backfired."

"Is he in danger?" Alarm peals through her words.

"Ah… yes, probably." It's not fair to lie to her. "But you're in more danger." I know how this shit works. I'm usually the guy shaking people down for money. They'll leave Zane free and hold his sister hostage for payment.

I hustle her down the stairs, my hand on the pistol in my waistband in case we meet anyone along the way. "I will help Zane when I know you're safe," I promise reluctantly. The douche doesn't deserve saving, but I can't stand Chelle being frantic over his safety.

Besides, the danger to her won't end until Zane's problem is solved.

I get her into my car and take off, going zero to sixty in under four seconds—my favorite reason for having a Tesla.

"I'm sorry, Chelle," I say. I don't want to apologize. I want to blame it all on Zane, but he's right. I played a part in this shit.

I feel her golden-eyed gaze on the side of my face but don't look because I'm weaving in and out of cars, racing to get back to the Kremlin where Chelle will be safe.

"What are you sorry for?" Her voice is a hoarse whisper, like she's terrified of hearing my answer.

"Involving you," I say. "I never would have hurt you, *zayka*. I don't harm the innocent. But I made Zane think I would. Now he's acted out of desperation to save you from me."

She lets out an audible breath. "What did he do?" The break in her voice kills me.

"I don't know." I grind my teeth. "I'm going to find out, and I will take care of it. I'll protect you both."

Chelle drags in a terraced breath and then lets out a whimper, like she's trying to keep from crying.

"I'm sorry," I repeat because hearing her anguish makes me want to burn this entire city down.

When I get her home, she gets in the shower, and I try to call Zane, but the little asshole doesn't pick up. I call one of our soldiers and ask him to go over to Chelle's place and fix the door. "Bring back-up," I warn.

Chelle stays in the shower so long I figure she's turned into a raisin. I enter the bathroom and push open the glass door to my huge walk-in shower. She's huddled under the water, her shoulder propped against the tile wall. She's not crying, but she looks lost.

"*Zayka*," I murmur and strip out of my clothes to join her. I've fucked her in this shower before. Taken her roughly against these walls. But this time is different. This time I just hold her. I hold her and kiss her head. And after a stretch, I maneuver her under the spray and wash her hair.

"Nikolai," she moans the way she does when we're having sex, only this time it sounds more broken. Lost.

"It's okay, Freckles. Everything is going to be okay."

"Is it?" She turns and searches my face, and I know she's asking about more than Zane. She's asking something about us, only I don't know what the question is, so I don't know how to answer.

Does she want us to be something more?

Could she be with a man like me?

Or is she saying she can't do this anymore? I saw the way she stared at the gun in my hand, like she was terrified to see it. Like it was a snake that might bite her, rather than a tool to protect her.

I pick up the bar of soap and run it over her breasts, soaping them until she moans and falls against me for a different reason. I slide it down her belly, soap her ass, then squat to soap both her legs. Then I pin her against the shower wall and lick her until she screams.

When her orgasm is over, I pick her up and carry her out of the shower. I sit her on the counter and grab a towel from the rack.

"Everything is going to be okay, little bunny," I promise, wrapping her and drying her soft skin. I'll pay off Zane's debts. I won't let anyone touch you. I promise."

"Why?" Chelle asks.

I should tell her.

I should explain what she means to me. That she's the light in the dark corridor. She's the magnetic axis I want to orbit around. She fills the vacuous spaces of my life.

I should say, "For you, Chelle."

But I don't.

I guess she's right. I do hold my cards close to my chest. Because I don't want to show her my hand. The one that's all hearts. And they're all for her.

Instead, I just leave her there in the bathroom to go

and find us something for dinner. I let her decipher me all on her own.

If she can.

CHELLE

I try calling Zane, but he doesn't answer, so I text instead. *What is happening? To whom do you owe money now?*

When he doesn't answer, I try again. *Nikolai will pay them off.*

I don't even think twice about getting in deeper with Nikolai. I don't want to unpack it right now, but I'm probably secretly relieved our thirty days might not be over in less than two weeks. That I might owe him more.

Because I love the way he exacts his due from me.

This time Zane replies. *Are you crazy? I was trying to get the money to pay the bratva off. I hate what you're doing for me.*

Grr. Logically, his response makes sense, but it brings up a huge wall of defensiveness. Fuck. Him. I chose to do this, and I told him I was fine. I hate the way he makes it feel icky. Sordid and shameful and wrong.

I hate all of it.

No, that's not necessarily true. I don't hate being here. I don't hate what I have with Nikolai.

Except, what do I have? The guy just held and washed me with total kindness in the shower, but he's basically bought—well, rented me—for a month. We have an expiration date. So I don't really *have* anything.

I write back, *I don't hate it.*

Zane texts, *???*

I start to text, *Nikolai is* and then stop. Nikolai is what? Not so bad? Wonderful? Good to me?

That's when it hits me full force. I've been resisting this

whole time, but it was useless: I'm falling in love with Nikolai.

The thought strikes new anxiety in me, sharp and electrifying. Different from the gut-churning worry over Zane. This is a full-throttle out-of-control sensation that zings from my scalp to the soles of my feet. I can't be with Nikolai.

I can't.

It's not possible. I'm a good girl. I have a college degree and a career as a junior publicist. I'm going places. I'm not going to—*I can't*—mix with the Russian bratva.

I can't.

I won't.

But I type it anyway because Zane should understand that I trust Nikolai. *Nikolai is good to me.*

He must trust Nikolai on some level, too, because he wanted him to protect me from the people who trashed my apartment.

Zane doesn't answer, but I experience a trickle of relief at having explained. Zane will let Nikolai pay his debt. This one crisis can be solved.

The other one—the one about my foolish heart—can be dealt with later.

19

Nikolai

The next day, we meet up in Ravil's office. Ravil provided a couple apartments in the building to the former slaves and Svetlana, Natasha's mom, who is a nurse midwife, has offered them medical care. Nadia and Adrian interviewed them to see what could be gleaned about how they ended up in the U.S.

"It was Poval," Adrian spits, pacing around the office like a caged animal. "Same operation that took Nadia. They came on shipping containers across the ocean then were trucked to Chicago."

"Anything you can find about the actual shipping containers could help me trace the money," Dima says from the laptop screen. "But I also may have a lead on finding Poval."

Adrian stops and swings his head in the direction of the screen. "What lead?"

"He has a daughter. She's in college in the U.K."

"What is her name?" Adrian's cuts across the room with deadly precision.

Dima hesitates, his gaze meeting Ravil's through the screen. Everyone in this office knows what Adrian will do with that information.

But she's an innocent. A young woman, like Nadia, who probably has nothing to do with her father's criminal empire.

I don't think Adrian would harm her. He's too protective of women for that. But he would probably use her for leverage. Just like I'd used Chelle.

Ravil inclines his head.

"I'll send you the information," Dima promises.

CHELLE

The next day, I head out of my building to wait for my Russian chauffeur/bodyguard. Nikolai wanted me to call in sick to work, but I refused. There was way too much work to be done, and Janette's not the type of boss who lets you work from home. She likes to do things in person.

I did promise not to go out to lunch, and I texted him an hour before I was ready to be picked up in the evening.

Traffic seems to be stalled in front of our building with construction. I scan the cars for his red Tesla.

My phone beeps with an incoming text. I reach for it in my purse at the same time something hard presses in my back.

"Scream and you're dead." The rough male voice behind me is unfamiliar.

My fingers close around my phone, and I hold it tight, my mind racing to formulate a plan.

"I'll take that." He reaches in my purse and pries the phone from my fingers. "Turn left and walk quickly to the corner." He jabs the gun against my kidney.

I stall, still scanning for Nikolai.

"*Now* or I shoot you right here in the street."

Stubbornness kicks in. "You wouldn't," I say. "You need me alive."

"Move or your punk-ass brother dies." The guy grasps the back of my hair and uses it to propel me to the corner.

His words make my feet move, even though I'm pretty sure I should just fight here on the street where I have a better chance of getting away.

"Where is Zane?" I demand.

"He's in the white van. If you want him to stay alive, you'll get in quietly with him."

They definitely know the right buttons to push. I'm not about to fight if Zane is right there and needs me.

The van door opens, and I see two guys in it but not Zane. I try to stop moving, but it's too late. Something hard cracks down on the back of my head and everything goes black.

≈

Nikolai

I'M CRAWLING the glass ceiling of my Tesla because there's goddamn construction or something on the blocks around Chelle's office, and I can't get through to pick her up.

I don't like it. There's an itchy feeling crawling up the back of my neck, especially because Zane hasn't answered his phone all day, and Dima couldn't track it—like he turned it off, or it's dead.

I put an actual tracker that can't be turned off in Chelle's phone last night after she went to bed, so at least I have that. Zane's safety is unfortunately as important to me as Chelle's because I don't want her to be damaged over something that happens to him.

I text Chelle to tell her to wait inside the building until I can get there, but she doesn't text back.

I try calling, but she doesn't answer.

That prickly feeling in full force, I pull up the tracking software. It looks like she's standing in front of her building.

Dammit.

I try calling again. When she still doesn't answer, I lose my shit. I swerve to drive with two wheels up on the sidewalk, forcing pedestrians to scatter for their lives.

Cars honk. People scream. I don't give a fuck.

I skid around the corner, finally making it to the street Chelle's building is on. I scan the sidewalk in front as I cut up onto the curb.

She's not fucking there.

She's not here, and my tracker says she is.

Blyad!

I throw the car in park and leap out, racing to the sidewalk, dialing Chelle again as I follow the tracker to the corner.

I hear the phone ring faintly beneath my feet.

I swallow the bile in my throat as I slowly look down to see the faint glow of her phone beneath the bars of the storm drain.

Goddamnit. *Chyort voz'mi!*

I jog back to the Tesla to the serenade of a dozen car horns and get in. I've never been particularly violent, but in this moment, I turn deadly. I will fucking kill every last one of those *zhopas* who touched Chelle.

She belongs to me and no one fucking touches what's mine.

I call Dima first, even though he's not here.

"They fucking took her!" I bellow.

"*Blyad'*. What happened?" His voice is low and urgent to match mine.

"Her phone is in the storm drain in front of her office. There was a jam-up on her street, and I couldn't get through. They probably caused the delay on purpose to stake her out."

"Fuck. Okay, I'm hacking the phone records to get both Chelle's and Zane's last calls and texts. It will just be a minute. While I do that, I'm going to connect in Ravil," he says smoothly, which is probably good thinking, but I hate our *pakhan* witnessing my total combustion. "Hang on one second."

A moment later he comes back. "I have Ravil and Maxim on the line too."

"Where are you, Nikolai?" Ravil asks.

"Driving to Zane's dorm. I've already been there today, as well as to Chelle's to check on the new locks and make sure the place wasn't being watched, but I didn't find anything."

"I'll send some guys to stay at Chelle's," Ravil says. "Text me the address."

"I have their last texts," Dima interrupts. "Chelle's was to you at 5:34 p.m. Zane's was to Chelle at 7:42 p.m. last night. He sent no other texts or calls before his phone went dark at 9:03 p.m. Do you want me to try to retrieve the contents of Zane's texts?"

Fuck. I doubt they have anything useful, but I mutter, "*Da*," anyway.

"Stand by."

"Let's talk this through," Maxim says. "If Zane owes this drug dealer money, he's going to use Chelle for leverage, no?"

I want to scream, *no shit*, but I manage to say, "Yes," through gritted teeth.

"He won't keep Zane once he has her. If he even has him now."

"Probably true," I grunt.

"Zane won't run if they have his sister, right?"

"No. He's a coward, but he wouldn't do that to her."

"This is good," Dima says. "Zane's phone stores everything in the cloud. I'm going to activate a new phone with his data, and it will be like having a duplicate. We can see everything—everywhere he's been, who he's talked to, all of it."

I let out the breath I'd been holding. Thank fuck for Dima and his super powers.

"Last text was from Chelle. She said… mm."

"*She said what?*" I shout at my dashboard as I double park in front of Zane's dorm. This is no fucking time to hold back shit from me.

"She said you would pay his debt and that you're good to her," Dima says quietly, and I suddenly understand his discretion.

My heart cinches up so tight I fear it will pop. I can't breathe, and it feels like my eyeballs are on fire.

"That was the last text?" I croak. I don't know why I'm suddenly so broken.

"Yes."

My brain stops. I can't think my way out of the car, much less out of this situation.

Fortunately, Maxim still has a functioning cortex. "Then Zane will come to you if and when he can," he reasons.

The thought brings me a small measure of relief. "Yes. He would come to me," I agree.

"I'll let Maykl know to be on the lookout," Maxim says.

"All right, let's dig into his locations," Dima says. "How far back should I go?" He starts reading off locations.

"Hold on," Maxim says. "What was that last one?"

Dima repeats it.

"That's close to where we met the Devil Dawgs to buy the women," Maxim says. "You think his drug dealers are the same assholes keeping slaves?"

"A coincidence, yes, but that would fit," I say. "He said he had a deal going, but it went wrong. The Devil Dawgs would be the kind to go in heavy."

"Since when is Zane a drug dealer?" Maxim asks. "I thought he was just a recreational coke user."

"I imagine he was trying to clear his debt with us," I grumble. I throw the Tesla into drive and pull back out. "I'm going to that warehouse. I know where it is."

"Not without us, you're not," Ravil snaps with an authority he doesn't often use.

When I don't answer, Maxim says, "We'll meet you there. Do not go in until we arrive."

I still don't answer because there's no fucking way I will sit and wait outside a warehouse for backup if I think Chelle is inside suffering.

"Nikolai, I will bring cash to pay off the debt. No one has to die," Maxim reasons. "If you go walking into their lair alone and get yourself killed, Chelle will be no better off."

"I'll wait," I grudgingly agree. "Make it fast."

"We've got your back. Just hold tight."

20

Chelle

Turns out, Zane wasn't in the van they threw me in, but he *is* in their warehouse. When the three guys from the van drag me and my aching head into some kind of warehouse, I see him curled up on the painted concrete floor. He has fresh bruising and blood all over his swollen face. His lip is cut, and it looks like the fingers of one hand have been broken.

The place is set up like a clubhouse. A makeshift bar stretches along one side. Empty beer bottles litter the tables. There's a pool table and dart boards set up, but also giant motorcycles parked inside. They're some kind of motorcycle club, I think.

Russian *mafiya* and motorcycle gangs. My brother really knows how to pick his business partners.

"We got the sister," the guy who grabbed me outside my building announces.

With the three guys who brought me, there's seven guys total. They're dressed in leather vests and covered in facial hair and tattoos.

"You hear that, boy? We found your big sister."

"You mean *little* sister," another one snickers. "I'll bet she's *real tight*."

"Don't hurt her." Zane struggles to his feet with great effort, wheezing at the pain. "I'll get your money right now."

"He will," I promise, hope kindling the moment I think of Nikolai and his pledge to pay it off. "He can get it. Or I can get it. Let me go, and I'll bring you everything he owes. How much is it?"

"Oh no, this one stays." One of the guys wraps a thick arm around my waist and picks me up. I kick my legs, struggling to get free. "We're going to have fun with her until you get back," he says darkly.

"No!" both Zane and I yell.

I claw at the arm around me, send my elbow backward into a paunchy gut. "Get your hands off me," I snarl. "Touch me, and you die." I continue to thrash, and the guy throws me to the ground and gives me a hard kick in the gut with his steel-toed boot.

I yelp like a wounded dog and wrap my arms around my stomach, wheezing with pain. The moment I can breathe again, I stagger to my feet. No way I'm going to curl up in a ball and take this shit. If they try to rape me, I will gouge their eyes out and kick their balls blue.

"Stop! It's true," Zane wheedles. "Her boyfriend is in the Russian bratva. He will kill everyone here if anything happens to her. You've heard of, of…Nikolai?" When their faces remain blank, he tries again. "O-oleg? Maxim!"

One of the men sneers. "He knows some Russian names."

Some others shrug.

"Yeah, we're shaking in our boots," another says.

The man who took me points a pistol at Zane. "Better

run, boy. Bring those Russians back while there's something left of her to save." He grabs my upper arm and drags me backward against his body, bringing one hand to paw my breast.

Zane's eyes are wild and terrified. He's as scared out of his mind as I am. He backs toward the door, holding my gaze. I read his apology in his eyes. His promise to do everything he can.

And because he's my little brother and I'm supposed to be the one taking care of him, I call out, "I'm fine. Just get Nikolai!"

~

Nikolai

I cruise down the street a block behind the warehouse, not wanting to pull right in and announce myself. Of course, there's nowhere in this neighborhood where parking a brand new Tesla would be inconspicuous. I end up angling it behind a dumpster.

I pull a spare pistol and clip out of the glove box and check both weapons for ammo. Then I get out, a pistol in each hand, and march toward the building.

When I see a figure emerge, I hold my gun straight out and point it at his head, still walking swiftly toward him.

The guy is half-running, half-limping, looking behind him like he's being chased.

Fuck.

"Zane."

"*Nikolai.* Oh thank God, you're here." He run-limps toward me, desperation and relief pouring from him. He looks horrible—much worse than when we worked him over. "How did you find us?"

Us. Thank fuck. "Where is she?"

Zane whirls and points wildly at the warehouse. "She's in there. We have to go back now. They were going to... they—"

I let out a string of Russian expletives and run toward the warehouse. I hear Zane's footfalls behind me.

I may have thought my days of violent crime were mostly in my past, but I was wrong.

I don't give a fuck about my soul. I will blast every last motherfucker in there.

"Wait, wait, wait," Zane pants behind me. "There's a lot of them. Seven, I think. You gotta wait. Where's Oleg?"

I turn. "You know how to shoot a gun?" I ask.

He shrugs. "Sort of." I hand him one of the pistols. "Shoot to kill," I advise. "Chest or head."

He draws in a breath and nods resolutely.

I stride up to the warehouse. "Which door?" I demand.

"Straight ahead," Zane says from behind me, and I march to it. Kick it open with my foot.

I hear Chelle screaming and white hot rage explodes inside me. Three men are bent over her, struggling to keep her down as she fights like a wildcat.

I take aim and fire. One. Two. Three dead.

Someone closer to me draws a weapon, and I gun him down too.

A guy with a shotgun fires at me and misses. I take him out at the same time another weapon fires.

Two bodies drop.

Zane's shell-shocked face tells me he just made his first kill.

Something hard hits my head and glass splinters around my face. I whirl and fire my gun.

Seven dead.

I scan the place for anyone else breathing as I jog toward Chelle.

"Watch my back," I tell Zane as I tuck the pistol in my waistband and lunge to free her from the bodies.

"It's okay, Chelle. I've got you." I throw them off her and haul her to her feet and against my body. She sobs, but struggles against me, so I release her. She looks at Zane, gun still in hand. Both of them wear the same horrified expressions. She looks at me. Then at the bodies strewn around the room.

"Don't look." I glance at Zane. "Take her out of here." I need to make sure things are buttoned up.

Still sobbing, she staggers for the door.

"Chelle!" Zane calls after her, following.

I hear the sound of tires on asphalt outside. "Wait, Chelle!" I pull my gun and jog after them, but it's just my brothers.

I hear Maxim's voice calling, "Chelle? Are you all right? Nikolai sent us. —Oh." He sees me. "What's the status?"

"Ready for clean up." I should have said it in Russian because Chelle whirls to face me, her expression even more shocked. She's pale, making a bruise on her cheek stand out. I want to kill the fuckers all over again for doing that to her. I want to burn the place down. Which is probably what Adrian will do with it. Arson is his preferred method of destruction.

She looks at the gun in my hand, and I hastily put it away.

"Talk to me, *zayka*. What do you need?" This time I'm smart enough not to touch her. I give her space but stay close.

She swallows. Her teeth chatter. "I need to be away from… all this." She flaps her hand at the warehouse. "From you."

I stand very still, trying to catch up to her thoughts.

"Chelle, I had nothing to do with that. Those guys were sex traffickers and drug dealers. They took you because Zane owed them from a drug deal gone wrong."

"Oh, God." Her eyes well with tears. "This is all too much. Zane just shot someone. You killed I don't know how many people in there. Like a professional."

Six people. And I suppose I am a professional, but I don't tell her that.

"This…" She shakes her head, sending tears streaming in several directions down her cheeks. "I can't unsee. I need to be away from this stuff. I can't do it. I can't do any of it."

"Do what?" I press against my better judgement. She's in shock. This isn't the time to have the relationship talk I thought we'd have at the end of her thirty days.

She turns to me, lips trembling. "Will you please take me home?"

There's a lot to read into those words, and I'm fairly sure I get the full meaning.

She's not coming back to my place. Not tonight.

Not ever.

I work to swallow around the tight band cinching my throat. "Yeah. Okay." I glance at Zane, still with my gun in his hand. Looking as broken and lost as she does. "This time I think Zane really does need a hospital, but I'll take him."

"Oh, God. No…"

Zane, hearing his name, walks closer. I take the gun from him and say firmly, "I'm going to take your sister home, and then we'll get you to a hospital. Come with me."

"I should go to the hospital, too," Chelle says weakly.

"You're going home." I place my hand on her back

and gently lead her away from the building. "Unless you have injuries that need to be looked at."

She touches the back of her head but just says in a small voice, "I want to go home."

The three of us are dead silent on the ride to her apartment. I'm still in crisis mode, my emotions overridden by adrenaline, my brain only focused on what needs to be done.

Zane tries to apologize to Chelle a couple times, but she doesn't answer him.

"I'll walk you up," I say when we get there.

"No," she says too sharply. Too quickly. "Please. Please just get Zane to the hospital."

I want to say a thousand things. Tell her that she means more than the money Zane owes. That I love her. That she means everything.

But I don't say any of them. Now is not the time.

I should have told her those things before we got to this moment, so she had something to hold onto.

But now she has nothing. I'm just the mobster who lured her brother to the dark side and almost got her raped or killed. I'm the killer who gunned down six men in a warehouse. I'm the guy who bought her for a month.

I'm nothing.

I should tell her I'll bring her things by, but I don't want to go there either. I don't want any words between us that make it officially over.

So I say nothing.

I just wait for the door to shut and drive away.

At the hospital, I want to be a dick and drop Zane at the door because this shit storm is all his doing, but I can't.

He's her brother and as lost as she is.

If I can't take care of her right now, at least I can take care of him.

21

Chelle

I go to work the next day like nothing happened. Like everything's normal in my world. I told Janette I got the bruise from running into the doorframe when I got up to go to the bathroom in the middle of the night.

Zane texted me at two in the morning to tell me his hand requires surgery.

I didn't reply. I had zero fucks left to give about Zane's situation.

I know I should be grateful to Nikolai for getting me and Zane out of his mess. I *am* grateful.

Except the gratitude rips my heart to shreds. I don't want to feel anything for him.

I want to write this whole thing off.

Pretend it never happened. Move on and never, ever look back.

I can't have this level of drama in my life. I don't run with motorcycle clubs or drug dealers. I definitely shouldn't run with the Russian *mafiya*. Not with killers who can single-handedly gun down a room of armed and dangerous men.

Nikolai let me walk away, but I don't know if it's over.

Our deal was thirty days or nothing, but I don't care. I'm out, regardless. Zane can figure out his own shit.

I'm officially done.

It's not like Nikolai didn't try to warn me off in the first place. He told me not to bail Zane out.

Well, I guess I had to learn in the hardest way possible.

I will never, ever allow myself to be in a situation like I was at that warehouse again.

I can't be in bed with a killer, no matter how great the orgasms.

I can make it through the day. And then I'll make it through the next one.

Eventually I'll allow myself to feel again, and this will all be over.

Nikolai

I text Chelle the next afternoon. *Are you okay?*

She doesn't reply.

I start to text *Can we talk?* but I delete the message before I hit send. I already know where this is going. Chelle is done. Pretending otherwise would only delay the pain. And yeah, maybe I could talk her into prolonging what we have—or had—but at the end of it all, she's not going to stay with me.

She only agreed to be with me because of a bargain we made.

Fuck. It feels like my heart just shriveled up and died inside my chest. Just when I found what felt like my new purpose in life, I fucked it up.

I close my eyes, trying to push away the torrent of fresh memories we made the last few weeks. Chelle, drunk, tugging me into her apartment and begging me to spank her. Showing up at my game full of piss and vinegar. The way she looked tied to my chair. The smiles she tossed over her shoulder when we rode bikes along the lake. The way she filled my kitchen. My apartment.

Goddammit. I wanted the real deal, and I'd found it.

I fucking love Chelle.

But that means I have to let her go. I care too much about her to push when she wants out, even though walking away feels like it will kill me.

I ache right down to my soul, so I drink a bottle of vodka on an empty stomach and when that's gone, I order one of our soldiers to bring me more and crash on the couch.

I intend to drink until I forget she was ever here.

CHELLE

I need to get my stuff from Nikolai's, but I'm not ready to see him. I'm still pretending to myself that nothing's wrong. That every day is normal, just like all the days I had before I met Nikolai.

I do double workouts at my spin gym and make an excuse to skip Wednesday at the Red Room, and I send Shanna vague texts about being busy. I don't want to—I can't—be with anyone who will talk about feelings. I'm working very hard not to have any.

On Sunday afternoon, Shanna shows up at my door with two grocery bags of brunch food.

"What are you doing here?" I ask, stepping back.

"You need me. I can tell." She gives me a critical look,

taking in the faded bruise on my face, then pushes past me and into my kitchen to start unloading. I follow her but can't make myself move to help or to speak.

She pops a champagne bottle, pours us mimosas and puts coffee cake and fruit salad on plates for us. "Come on," she says, picking up her mimosa and plate. "Tell me what's going on."

"How do you know I need you?" I ask, mechanically picking up my plate and glass and following.

"You're doing robot-Chelle. This is how you were after your dad died. What happened?" She eyes the bruise again. When I don't answer, she asks very quietly, "Did Nikolai do that?"

I shake my head miserably. "It's a really long story."

"That's why we have champagne. I've got you, sister. Spill."

I set my plate and fork down on the coffee table and straighten my back. "Maybe it's not that long. Here's that short version. Zane couldn't stand me having sex with Nikolai to pay off his debt, so he somehow got into bed with a motorcycle club—I think selling drugs, but I'm not sure. I don't even want to know. Then things went bad— again, I don't know how, and they came and trashed my apartment and kidnapped me." My voice breaks on the word *kidnapped*.

Dang it. I was trying to keep it together.

Shanna sets her champagne down and pulls me into a hug. "Jesus, Chelle. That's terrifying. Then what happened?"

"Zane was there, and he was all beat up. They let him go. He was going to get money from Nikolai to buy me back."

The trauma of that night blows through me full force.

This was what I was resisting all week. The fear. The helplessness. The violation.

I choke on a sob.

Shanna squeezes my hand.

"They were going to rape me," I sob, touching the bruise on my face I got while fighting with them.

Shanna wraps me in the tightest hug imaginable. I bawl into her shoulder, wetting her Beatles t-shirt. "But they didn't?" she asks softly.

"No." I pull back and wipe my nose. "Because Nikolai came in with Zane and they, um, killed everyone."

I know Shanna was trying to play it cool, not screeching about my bruise, waiting for me to tell the story, but her eyes widen now. "Wow. Okay. Shit."

"Yeah." I cry some more, but it feels better now that I've told someone.

Like holding in that terrible secret was burning my insides like battery acid.

"So did the police come? What happened then?"

"No." A fresh sob rips through me, remembering. "Nikolai's friends showed up, and he said it was *ready for cleaning*." I make air quotes with the last three words. "It really scared me."

"Oh, babe." She squeezes my arm and doesn't let go. "Scared you because you saw into his world?"

I nod, tears streaming down my face. "I asked him to take me home, and I broke off our arrangement. My stuff is there, and I don't want to call him to get it, and I don't know how Zane's going to pay him back, and I don't even care."

"Well, I can go get your stuff, so don't worry about that. I'm thinking the Zane thing doesn't matter. I mean… Nikolai rescued you, Chelle. He killed a bunch of guys for you. I think that means he cares."

Hearing her say it out loud settles me. The white panic of seeing Nikolai as a killer fades, and he becomes an outline of the man I know. I nod. "Yeah. I guess… I guess I knew the whole time he would rescue me. I mean, I… expected it."

That thought brings another wave of relief. Talking this all out is helping release the dam of trauma. My brain just shut off at the warehouse. The wires disconnected. Shorted out.

Now they're starting to rewire.

"Yeah. I mean, I met Nikolai. I liked him. He seemed like a sweetheart and totally into you. I'm not going to be sad that he killed guys who were trying to rape you. I'm just not." She shrugs.

Hearing her absolve him lightens the air around me. "Yeah."

"I mean, what are you really upset about here? That some guys who probably deserved it got killed or that things are over with Nikolai?"

A shudder of recognition runs through my body, and I drag in a hiccupped breath. "I miss Nikolai," I admit as the full realization hits me. I'm grieving. Not over what happened to me, but the choice I made afterward.

"So maybe talk to him?" Shanna suggests. "Tell him what freaked you out. I don't know what he's into. How bad it is. But maybe you could—I don't know—set some hard limits, and it could work."

My stomach churns some more. Could it work? Could I be with someone like Nikolai long-term? Get married and have kids with a guy who's killed men?

I scrub my hands over my face. I'm getting ahead of myself, as usual. "I don't even know if he's that into me. I mean, we had no discussions of what would happen beyond the thirty nights. Maybe killing for someone isn't a big deal to a guy like him."

Shanna rolls her eyes. "Will you just call him? You can't figure this one out all by yourself in your own head." She hands me my phone.

I stare at it for a moment, heart pounding, then dial his number.

He doesn't answer, and there's no voicemail. An uneasy feeling stirs in my belly.

Maybe it's too late.

I text, *Sorry I bailed. I was scared. Can we talk?* and hit send.

As soon as I do, I feel better. The weight on my chest lightens and shimmers of hope squirrel back in.

Maybe this doesn't have to be over.

There's still so much to work out—so much I'm afraid of—and yet the explosions of joy that thought brings can't be wrong.

I throw my arms around Shanna, and she hugs me back in a long, tight hug.

"You feel better?" she asks.

"Much. Thank you."

"I've got you, girl. Let's have some more champagne."

Nikolai

Dima shows up on Friday. At least I think he's actually here. It's hard to say. I've been either drinking or sleeping for the past two weeks.

I vaguely remember the guys coming and going—bringing food down and yelling at me or some such bullshit.

Dima seems pissed. He drags open the drapes in my bedroom.

Oh. I think Oleg's with him because somehow my bed lifts, and I roll out of it.

"Tebya yest khuy v sadnitse?" I grumble when I hit the floor.

"No, you're the one with the dick stuck up his ass. Get up." Yep, Dima is here. The two of them haul me to my feet. "It's Friday. You have to go run your game, or Ravil will have your ass. Let's go."

"Ravil can suck my dick," I mutter.

"Careful," Dima cautions as the two guys drag me to the shower.

I hate being in it because it reminds me of Chelle. Everything in this damn apartment reminds me of her. I should have moved back up to my bedroom upstairs when she left. I stay in a long time, but I manage to remain on my feet and get cleaned up, so I count it as a win.

When I stumble out, I find Dima and Oleg in my kitchen. They have a pile of sub sandwiches on the counter, which they are already eating.

"I have a table," I mutter, grabbing a sandwich.

"Yeah, it looks nice." Dima and Oleg follow me to sit at it.

"Chelle picked it out." I'm both simultaneously proud of the table she picked for me and pained by the memory of it. I unwrap the sandwich and take a bite.

"So what's going on with Chelle?" he asks.

I shrug. "She's done."

Turns out, I was starving. I attack the sandwich.

"She texted you five days ago asking to talk."

I stop chewing. "She did?" I ask with my mouth full.

Dima pushes my phone in front of my face, and I read

her message. The full brunt of pain returns. More than I can handle.

I shake my head. "It's not going to work." I resume chewing.

Dima gives Oleg a *what-the-fuck?* look.

"What is wrong with you? You haven't left your apartment in almost two weeks over this girl, and now you're not going to call her back when she asks to talk?"

"It's not going to work," I repeat. "She sees me as a murderer."

I don't want to keep chasing a woman who doesn't think I'm redeemable. It's not worth it.

Every player needs to know when to fold.

22

Chelle

On Friday, I call Story.

My hope withered during the week when Nikolai never texted me back.

Now this gnawing sense of panic that I've lost him grows stronger every day.

At least Zane came over, and we had a long, painful heart to heart about his bad choices this year. I guess the good thing is that he's been scared back to sanity. He swears he won't touch cocaine or gambling ever again.

I hope it's true.

He also told me Nikolai had stayed by his side the night at the hospital, driving him home at two in the morning. Which means Shanna's right. Nikolai cares.

Maybe he even loves me.

God, I definitely love him. I don't know how or why I kept pretending I didn't. Yes, I have qualms about his profession, but I actually have zero doubts about him, the person. I've always been able to trust him to do the right thing. He's had my back in every situation.

Too bad I didn't have his.

The fear that I've irreparably screwed things up tears me up. I don't even pretend to believe the tale I kept telling myself that he doesn't care. That it was just about sex. If he didn't care, he wouldn't have let me go. He wouldn't have sat with Zane in the hospital. He wouldn't have killed for me.

I give Story a call from work, pretending it's about getting the Storytellers booked at the Red Room.

"Chelle, I like you, but I'm not sure I can keep doing business with you now," she says flat-out.

My heart starts beating faster. "What do you mean?"

"I mean, I'm the type who's super loyal to her friends, and at the moment, my friend is hurting because of you."

I grip the edge of my desk for support. "Nikolai?" I croak. I try to find my voice. "He's hurting?"

"Straight up—you broke his heart. He's been holed up in his apartment drinking and sleeping for days. We've been bringing food down and checking just to make sure he's alive. We had to call his brother to come back to deal with him. It's not cool."

"He hasn't answered my text," I tell her miserably. "Should I... do you think I could come down there tonight? Would Maykl let me in?"

Story pauses, then says, "No, Oleg says they have poker night tonight. Maybe tomorrow."

No, not tomorrow. Every minute of the two of us being broken-hearted feels like an epic tragedy. "Where is the game?"

"That's probably not a good idea," Story says.

"Please. My heart is broken, too, Story. I need to work things out with him. I can't wait another day. Please?"

There's another pause, and then Story says, "Oleg says

you'd have to come before it starts. Like eight or eight-thirty."

"No problem. I'll be there. Where should I go?"

"He's going to text you the information when he gets it."

"Thank you. So much." I fight back tears because I hear Janette talking outside my new office. Losing it at work would be a bad thing.

It seems fitting that I'm going to the place where I first met Nikolai to start over.

At least I hope it's a do-over and not a *done*.

Nikolai

I feel like shit. Even though I showered, shaved and ate, my head aches, and my body feels like it's made of lead.

Adrian, Dima and Oleg set up for poker night at the hotel I picked last-minute while I stand at the window and look out.

I'm awash in desolation. This isn't the life I want to lead. This sense of emptiness. Purposelessness.

I don't know what to do with myself.

A knock sounds at the door, and for some reason, none of the other assholes move to answer it. "Who the fuck is it?" I demand, looking pointedly at Oleg.

He opens the door a crack and looks out, then looks at me and tips his head toward the door.

"Who?" I demand.

When he stares back at me without answering, I suddenly know.

My body lights on fire. I don't know if it's with anger or purpose. I stride to the door and yank it open.

Chelle looks kissable.

Fuckable.

Too damned cute.

I hate that I love her so much.

"What are you doing here?" I demand.

She pales, her big golden eyes trained on my face, her freckles standing out. "I, um, came to play poker with you."

I shake my head. "Go home." I start to go back inside, but she catches my hand and tugs me out into the hallway. The same place we began this whole thing.

"I was going to wager my body," she says quickly, like she's trying to get it out. She unbuttons her coat to show me her tits pushed up in a sexy little black bustier.

I'm shaking my head. We're not doing this again. No way.

"Because I already lost my heart," she blurts.

I go perfectly still. Swallow.

Then I lose my mind. I barrel into her and shove her up against the wall, claiming her mouth with a searing kiss.

I grab her ass and hoist her up, and she wraps her arms and legs around me, kissing me back.

"I'm sorry," she whimpers between kisses. "I'm sorry I left."

"I love you, Chelle," I tell her, even though it feels like jumping out of a plane with no chute. "I missed you so goddamn much." I grind the bulge of my erection in the notch between her legs as I kiss her neck, her jaw, her forehead. "But I don't want you back unless you're staying," I rasp.

She stares at me in shock. It's too much to ask, I know that. My girl thinks way too much about things, and she's already not sure about me and the bratva.

She sucks in a breath. "I want to," she whispers.

It's enough.

"I love you, Nikolai." There's more conviction in those words, and the grace of them bathes my body in comfort. In surrender.

That's more than enough. It's all we need. We love each other. The rest we can figure shit out.

"Come home with me," I murmur, and she nods. "Now?" she nods again.

I look at the door to the hotel suite.

Fuck them. They can handle the games.

I have my girl.

I carry Chelle into the elevator and hit the *down* button. She's mine now. No matter what, she's mine.

I won't let her go a second time.

23

Chelle

"I'm sorry I scared you," Nikolai murmurs. I'm wrapped in his arms in the elevator on the way up to his apartment.

"You didn't scare me," I say. "I scared myself. The situation scared me." The image of the dead bodies flickers in my mind, and I realize what tripped me into my freak-out. "I found my dad after he shot himself."

"Oh, Chelle." Nikolai cups half my face, while the other cheek remains pressed firmly against his chest. "I'm so sorry."

"I honestly think I'd blocked the image of it out until this moment. But the feeling was the same. The sickness and fear."

"I'm sorry, *zayka*." The elevator opens, and we step out. I look up at him. "You've seen a lot of death."

He nods.

"That scared me, too."

"I know. I…" He hesitates with his keycard against the lock. "My place is trashed. You should probably wait out here while I clean up quickly."

"It's fine." I push the door open. I don't know what he's talking about because the place is spotless.

"Oh." He blinks a few times. "My brothers are very good to me."

"*Brothers*, plural?"

"Bratva means brotherhood. They are all my brothers. This was very kind." He looks at me thoughtfully. "They knew you were coming tonight. Who told you where to come?"

"I called Story, and she told me she couldn't do business with me because I'd broken your heart. I told her my heart was broken too, and I needed to see you before it was too late."

Nikolai leans his forehead against mine. "I'm a lucky man."

"I'm luckiest."

The edges of Nikolai's mouth kick up. "In a minute, I'm going to take you in my bedroom and fuck you blind, but first I think we need to talk." He picks me up to straddle his waist again and carries me to an overstuffed armchair where he sits. "You have questions about what I am. What I do. I refused to answer them before, but I will answer anything now. One-time offer." He palms my ass and squeezes, making it hard for me to concentrate.

But he's right. I have questions that torment me about him.

But none of them come out. I don't really want to know the specifics after all.

He helps me. "I have done many things for the bratva, Freckles. But we operate with a code. We don't harm the innocent. We protect our own. We don't use drugs or sell flesh. There's some smuggling, a lot of tax evasion. Gambling and loan sharking, obviously. We use intimidation and fear to get our way in business negotiations but rarely actually have to deliver on the threats."

I blink at him. Nothing he says makes me panic, but I realize my real fears haven't been addressed. "Will you ever go to jail?"

He shakes his head. "Highly unlikely. Ravil is married to the best defense attorney in town. Besides, the cops have no reason to go after me."

"Can you leave it? Would you ever?" I leave off the *for me* part because I'm making the demand. I just want to know if he's locked in.

"Code says no, but two of my brothers are already halfway out. Our *pakhan* is unusually understanding. Arrangements can be made for anything, I believe."

I unbutton the top of his shirt. "If you hadn't met me, what would you have done to Zane?"

"I would've leaned on him until we came to a mutually agreeable solution," he says. "Like him signing over the Mustang."

I undo another button on his shirt.

"What else?" he asks. "What are you afraid of, Chelle?"

"I was afraid you only wanted me for sex."

He clicks his tongue. "Here I thought that's what you were using me for."

I laugh—a relieved sort of belly laugh that releases all the remaining tension in my body. "Well, that's true. But only because I didn't think I could handle the bratva thing."

"And now?" He arches a sexy brow.

"Now I feel better about it."

"Move in with me."

RENEE ROSE

"Okay."

His wide, white-toothed smile is a brilliant reward. "I want you to know my friends."

"The bratva?"

"Yes. And their wives. The whole gang. You will like them."

The possibility of belonging slides over and lands on my shoulders. Since my father's suicide, I've felt so alone. Like it was just me and Zane against the world. No family or safety net, other than Shanna, who is also quite alone.

The prospect of becoming part of Nikolai's tight-knit family feels like a return to home, even though I haven't met them all yet.

"What else, little bunny? What do you need to know before I punish you for leaving me?"

My nipples tighten at his words. "Nothing," I whisper.

His fingers tighten on my ass.

"What's my punishment?"

His lids droop. "I haven't decided yet."

I roll my hips over his. "Wait," I say. "Maybe one more thing."

He pulls my hips to continue the motion I stopped, grinding me over his erection. "What is it?"

"You're serious about us? Committed?"

"I'm all in, Freckles."

I smile at him and crawl down onto my knees on the floor, working open the button on his pressed slacks.

"Mm. That's a good start," Nikolai rumbles.

I release his erection and grip the base to steady it for my mouth. "Why me?" I ask, the moment before I lick around the head of his cock.

He shivers at the contact. "Are you asking what I love about you, little bunny?"

"Mmm hmm." I drag out the humming sound as I take

224

him deep into the pocket of my cheek. His cock surges in my mouth, growing thicker.

He sucks in his breath and groans before responding. "I love… your golden lioness eyes. And your freckles. I love your fire and determination, especially because it comes in such a small, adorable package."

I take him in and out of my mouth with long, slow pulls, drinking in his words and rewarding him for them.

He wraps his fist in my hair but doesn't pull. "I love this long, thick hair. I love how buttoned up tight you are because it's so fun when you finally let go."

I take him deep to the back of my throat, concentrating on relaxing so I can take him deeper.

"I love the way you trust me. That you like to be spanked. I love when you dance around in your kitchen in your panties."

"Whaff?" I pull off him and stare in shock. "What did you say?"

Nikolai has the grace to look rueful. "Did I mention my brother is one of the best hackers to ever come out of Russia?"

I straighten my back. "Are you telling me…" My mind reels as it puts the pieces together. "My Echo! Were you spying on me through my Echo?"

Nikolai catches my wrist and tugs it to his lips, kissing my pulse. "Just once. The morning after we made our deal."

My face probably turns a shade of crimson based on how hot it gets. "Oh my God." I try to cover it with my hands, but he catches my other wrist and holds it fast. "I'm so embarrassed."

"That is the moment I fell hopelessly in love with you, Chelle Goldberg."

"Oh God," I moan.

"I'll make you deal." Nikolai's eyes crinkle.

"What is it?"

"Give me a repeat show, and I'll forget about your punishment."

My lips twist into a rueful smile. "I might prefer the punishment," I admit.

He laughs. "You would, wouldn't you? How about this? Dance for me, and your brother's slate is clean. I was going to make you restart your thirty nights."

"I thought you were all in. Forever. No end date."

"Oh, I am. But that doesn't mean I won't keep you as my slave forever."

I laugh, happiness bubbling everywhere because the idea excites me to no end. "So which do you want, the dance or the blowjob?" I purr, dropping my gaze to his erection.

"Both." He pulls his phone out of his pocket to boot the song up. "Dance for me, Freckles."

The music comes out of his speaker in the kitchen, filling the apartment. I stand, pumping my hips to the beat in my version of a twerk as I give him a strip tease. I shuck my bustier and unbutton my jeans. I time pulling them down with the lyrics, dropping to my lowest squat, bouncing on the floor to take them off before I snake back up.

Nikolai strokes his thumb across his lower lip, his heavy-lidded gaze pinned on me.

Feeling powerful, I dance around in my panties the way I had that day in my kitchen, giving him the best show I know how. When I start to get self-conscious again, I drop to the floor and crawl up to him to finish the job I started.

When I take him into my mouth again, he cradles my head with both hands. "This is what I've been missing my whole life," he rumbles appreciatively. "You. Dancing in my living room. Filling up the empty spaces in my life."

I pop off and give him a cheshire cat smile. "Sucking your dick?"

His smile is warm as he takes over, feeding his length back into my mouth. "Definitely sucking my dick."

EPILOGUE

Nikolai

Oleg, Adrian and I wait outside Zane's dorm for him.

"Oh shit. What is this?" He walks up with his hand in a brace with three of his fingers splinted from the surgery he had two weeks ago.

"How's your hand?" I ask, eyeing the brace.

He flips it over to look at it like it's a foreign object. "It's okay, I guess. It hurts, but I'm staying off the pain pills. I'm done with all that."

"That's good. I'll kick your ass if you go back to it."

"Thanks for the support," he says drily, but I see him flick a nervous glance Oleg's way.

I dangle the keys to his Mustang in front of him. "I came to offer you a deal," I say.

"You still have it!" He reaches for the keys, but I jerk them away.

"You haven't heard my terms yet."

"Okay." He splits a wary glance between me and the guys.

"I need your support."

A smirk shows around his lips. "Are you buying my affection?"

"Yeah. I want to lock down your sister."

His smile grows, which relaxes me. He doesn't still think I'm the worst thing to happen to Chelle.

"What do you need from me?"

"Come to the Red Room tomorrow night. Chelle's organized an event, and I'm going to pop the question there."

"I'll need a car to get there." Zane holds his hand out for his keys.

"That's my boy." I drop the keys into his palm. "Eight o'clock. Don't be late." We start to walk away.

"I'll be there."

"Oh—" I turn around and point at Zane. "if you tell her? I'll kill you."

He chuckles. "I believe you."

CHELLE

I bounce on my heels with excitement. Tonight's event was all my doing. I set up the gig for the Storytellers at The Red Room. I launched a social media campaign using both their Facebook, Instagram, Youtube and Tiktok accounts. I listed it in the local papers and online magazines. I arranged for a couple food trucks to park out front to make it even more of an event, and I even invited Janette to show her what I'm capable of.

She stands beside me now, sipping a whiskey sour and surveying the crowd. "Looks like you threw together a great event in just a few weeks," she says. "I can't wait to see how the launch with Skate 32 goes."

"I promise I did this all on my own time," I tell her.

"I wasn't worried about it," she tells me. "You're on salary, anyway, so it's not like I'm clocking your time."

Nikolai comes up and stands behind me, his hand lightly resting on my back in that gentle, yet possessive way he has. He's my rock. The one who makes all this seem easy and possible. But this event feels like my gift to him. A way to honor his friends and try to earn their respect, especially since I might not be their favorite person after the way I hurt him.

"Janette, this is my boyfriend, Nikolai. The band members are friends of his. And mine," I add, hoping it's true.

Nikolai shakes Janette's hand and drops a kiss on my head. "Chelle is a star for putting this together."

"She absolutely is. I'm going to go check on my food order at the food truck." Janette leaves, and Nikolai leads me to the bar to get a drink.

I look over as Nikolai's friends from the penthouse suite pour in. Oleg came in with the band, of course, but Sasha, a highly-entertaining redhead and her husband, Maxim, arrive. Adrian follows, with his sister, Nadia, who looks more than a little frightened to be here. When Flynn waves to her from where he's setting up on stage, she freezes in place, and looks behind her, as if to see if he's waving to someone else.

Flynn gets on the mic. "Nadia's in the house," he says, waving again.

A shy smile breaks out on her face. I haven't known her for long, but it's the first time I've seen her look anything but haunted. She lifts her fingers in a tiny wave.

Ravil and Lucy, Nikolai's boss and his wife, didn't come tonight because of their baby Benjamin, but Nikolai suspects they also stayed home because they're happy to have the penthouse to themselves for a change.

Over the past couple of weeks, I've gotten to know them all more. We've hung out in the penthouse to watch movies or share meals, and I had them down to Nikolai's for Sunday brunch a couple times. Dima and his girlfriend Natasha are often here on weekends, but they won't be here tonight, since it's mid-week.

The band starts up, keeping it more mellow than usual to go with the earlier happy hour vibe. Their regular fans, who we lured over from Rue's, love the change-up and cheer accordingly after each song.

I see Derek standing beside Shanna enjoying the music, and they both shoot me a thumbs-up.

When the song ends, Story gets on the mic. "Thank you all so much for coming out to see us and to the Red Room for hosting. This is our first gig here, and we're having an awesome time."

The crowd cheers.

"We also wanted to thank our friend Chelle for setting this up. Chelle, where are you?"

I wave my hand in the air.

"There she is, everyone. Somebody buy her a drink!"

Nikolai raises his hand and nods, and I laugh. He catches Shanna's attention, and she comes over with my usual dirty martini.

"This is fun!" she says as she hands it to me. "You did a great job. Derek loves the new crowd."

"Awesome." I pick up the toothpick of olives absently and realize it has a bow tied on the end. "What is this?"

Shanna gives me a wink and disappears to wait on someone else.

"What is this?" I repeat to Nikolai, stroking my fingers down the delicate ribbon ends.

His lips twitch.

"Did you do this?" I tug one of the ends and the bow

unravels, dropping a delicate gold ring onto the bar. I gasp. "Oh! Is this from you?"

A thin slip of paper is wrapped around the ring. I unwrap it and flatten it on the bar. Something is written in cyrillic letters.

I twist to look at Nikolai, whose expression is inscrutable. "What does it say?"

"*Ty moya*," he says, the corners of his lips curving up.

My heart beats faster as I examine the ring. It's both delicate and spectacular at the same time, with a thin band and six diamonds in a row. I slip it on the ring finger of my right hand and turn to face him fully, placing my hands on his sturdy chest. "What does that mean?"

He smirks. "You're mine." He takes the ring off my right hand and puts it on my left.

I laugh as giddy thrills of excitement bounce through me. "Is this your way of proposing?"

He nods. "*Da.*"

"Do I have a say in it?"

He shakes his head, but he's smiling, his gaze locked on mine. "*Nyet.*"

"Well," I murmur. "I guess you'd better kiss me then."

Nikolai moves in quickly, cupping my face and claiming my mouth in the kind of kiss I feel directly between my legs.

I hear a cheer go up behind Nikolai, and when I open my eyes, I realize the entire gang is crowded behind us. Sasha and Maxim, Oleg, Adrian and Nadia, my brother, Zane. Even Dima and Natasha are there.

"I take it she said *yes*?" Shanna asks from the other side of the bar just before she pops the cork on a bottle of champagne.

"I didn't give her a choice," Nikolai says.

Another cheer with shouts and laughter goes up from our crowd.

Story congratulates us from the stage, and the band starts a kick-ass version of Billy Idol's "White Wedding."

I pull Nikolai's face down for a kiss. "I love you," I murmur. "*Ty moya.*"

"*Ty moy,*" he corrects. "Yes, I am yours."

***

For a special New Year's Eve **Bonus Epilogue** with Chelle and Nikolai, join Renee's newsletter. If you enjoyed this book, please consider leaving a review. They make an enormous difference for indie authors.

Be sure to read the next book in the series, *The Cleaner.*

WANT MORE? THE CLEANER

Her father ruined my sister's life.
   Now she will have to pay the price.

Get *The Cleaner* now

WANT FREE RENEE ROSE BOOKS?

Go to http://subscribepage.com/alphastemp to sign up for Renee Rose's newsletter and receive a free copy of *Alpha's Temptation, Theirs to Protect, Owned by the Marine, Theirs to Punish, The Alpha's Punishment, Disobedience at the*

Dressmaker's and *Her Billionaire Boss*. In addition to the free stories, you will also get special pricing, exclusive previews and news of new releases.

OTHER TITLES BY RENEE ROSE

Chicago Bratva

"Prelude" in Black Light: Roulette War

The Director

The Fixer

"Owned" in Black Light: Roulette Rematch

The Enforcer

The Soldier

The Hacker

The Bookie

The Cleaner

Vegas Underground Mafia Romance

King of Diamonds

Mafia Daddy

Jack of Spades

Ace of Hearts

Joker's Wild

His Queen of Clubs

Dead Man's Hand

Wild Card

Contemporary

Daddy Rules Series

Fire Daddy

Hollywood Daddy

Stepbrother Daddy

Master Me Series

Her Royal Master

Her Russian Master

Her Marine Master

Yes, Doctor

Double Doms Series

Theirs to Punish

Theirs to Protect

Holiday Feel-Good

Scoring with Santa

Saved

Other Contemporary

Black Light: Valentine Roulette

Black Light: Roulette Redux

Black Light: Celebrity Roulette

Black Light: Roulette War

Black Light: Roulette Rematch

Punishing Portia (written as Darling Adams)

The Professor's Girl

Safe in his Arms

Paranormal
Two Marks Series

Untamed

Tempted

Desired

Enticed

Wolf Ranch Series

Rough

Wild

Feral

Savage

Fierce

Ruthless

Wolf Ridge High Series

Alpha Bully

Alpha Knight

Bad Boy Alphas Series

Alpha's Temptation

Alpha's Danger

Alpha's Prize

Alpha's Challenge

Alpha's Obsession

Alpha's Desire

Alpha's War

Alpha's Mission

Alpha's Bane

Alpha's Secret

Alpha's Prey

Alpha's Sun

Shifter Ops

Alpha's Moon

Alpha's Vow

Alpha's Revenge

Midnight Doms

Alpha's Blood

His Captive Mortal

All Souls Night

Alpha Doms Series

The Alpha's Hunger

The Alpha's Promise

The Alpha's Punishment

The Alpha's Protection (Dirty Daddies)

Other Paranormal

The Winter Storm: An Ever After Chronicle

Sci-Fi

Zandian Masters Series

His Human Slave

His Human Prisoner

Training His Human

His Human Rebel

His Human Vessel

ABOUT RENEE ROSE

USA TODAY BESTSELLING AUTHOR RENEE ROSE loves a dominant, dirty-talking alpha hero! She's sold over a million copies of steamy romance with varying levels of kink. Her books have been featured in USA Today's *Happily Ever After* and *Popsugar*. Named Eroticon USA's Next Top Erotic Author in 2013, she has also won *Spunky and Sassy's* Favorite Sci-Fi and Anthology author, *The Romance Reviews* Best Historical Romance, and *has* hit the *USA Today* list ten times with her Bad Boy Alpha and Wolf Ranch series, as well as various anthologies.

Please follow her on Tiktok

Renee loves to connect with readers!
www.reneeroseromance.com
reneeroseauthor@gmail.com

f facebook.com/reneeroseromance

🐦 twitter.com/reneeroseauthor

📷 instagram.com/reneeroseromance

ⓐ amazon.com/Renee-Rose/e/B008AS0FT0

BB bookbub.com/authors/renee-rose

Printed in the USA
CPSIA information can be obtained
at www.ICGtesting.com
CBHW021527010324
4848CB00040B/698